ID678910

Maggie's Story

Maggie's Story

thirsty

Tyndale House Publishers, Inc.
Carol Stream, Illinois

DANDI DALEY
MACKALL

Go to areUthirsty.com for more info.

TYNDALE is a registered trademark of Tyndale House Publishers, Inc.

thirsty[?] and the thirsty[?] logo are trademarks of Tyndale House Publishers, Inc.

Maggie's Story

Designed by Jacqueline Noe

Edited by Ramona Cramer Tucker

Scripture quotations are taken from the *Holy Bible,* New Living Translation,
copyright © 1996, 2004. Used by permission of Tyndale House Publishers, Inc.,
Carol Stream, Illinois 60188. All rights reserved.

Library of Congress Cataloging-in-Publication Data

Mackall, Dandi Daley.
  Maggie's story / Dandi Daley Mackall.
    p. cm.
  ISBN-13: 978-1-4143-0978-1 (pbk.)
  ISBN-10: 1-4143-0978-3 (pbk.)
  1. Mary Magdalene, Saint—Fiction. 2. Jesus Christ—Fiction. 3. Christian
women saints—Fiction. 4. Ohio—Fiction. I. Title.
PS3613.A27257M34 2006
813'.54—dc22   2005029348

Printed in the United States of America

10   09   08   07   06
7   6   5   4   3   2   1

*To Maureen Daley Pento,
my sister in life,
my sister in Christ*

Acknowledgments

I'm grateful to Tyndale House for catching the vision for this book, helping me develop it, and trusting me to write it. Thanks to Karen and Ramona, my amazing editors.

I think I've enlisted every family member and most of my friends to pray for this book. Thanks especially to my husband, Joe; to my kids, Jen, Katy, and Dan; to my sister, Maureen; and to my buddy Laurie, for prayerfully reading various drafts of *Maggie's Story*. I'm very blessed to have all of you. Thanks.

A Letter to Readers

This book is different from anything I've ever written, and I want to make it absolutely clear to readers that *Maggie's Story* is a work of fiction. I've simply tried to imagine what life might have been like if Mary Magdalene and Jesus and the disciples had lived closer to home, in our own decade, in my own state. I've invented dialogue, contemporary settings, characters, and events, as I've attempted to get inside the head of "Maggie." That's what fiction does.

Who was the real Mary Magdalene? What do we actually know about her? There are a lot of wild theories flying around about this woman. But most of the talk is as unfounded as the gossip heard in school hallways or around the watercooler.

The facts of Mary Magdalene's life are few, and they can all be found in the Gospels:

Fact: Mary Magdalene and other women traveled with Jesus and the disciples on occasion, as Jesus taught people about God and how they could relate with him.

Fact: Jesus "cast out seven demons," healing Mary. Her life was profoundly changed by Christ (Luke 8:1-3).

Fact: Mary Magdalene stayed by the cross during Jesus' crucifixion (John 19:25).

Fact: Mary Magdalene was among the first to go to Jesus' tomb and find it empty (John 20:1).

Fact: Mary stayed outside the tomb until she saw Jesus. She was the first to see the resurrected Christ (John 20:11-18).

Writing this book has been an amazing journey for me, as I've tried to imagine how Mary Magdalene's story might have played out today. If you want to read more about the life of Mary Magdalene and the actual events that inspired this book, I've included a Check It Out section on page 305. A search of the passages suggested there, chapter by chapter, will reveal the stories, facts, and encounters I've used for many of the events of *Maggie's Story*. You may want to use the Check It Out section to investigate the facts for yourself or as a basis for a study or discussion group.

Writing *Maggie's Story* drove me to examine the Bible's accounts—the real record—the only truth about Mary Magdalene, about Jesus, and about us.

I hope reading this story will do the same for you.

Part 1

Chapter One

Slayton, Ohio
Dear Chance,

I promised myself I was going to start
writing you whenever I could. I'll tell
you the straight truth, too, which is
more than most have done for me.

So here goes. Just for the record,
I'm pushing 22, although I've been told
more than once that I look 10 years
older than that. I've lived in Slayton,
Ohio, my whole life, and I've made it
my whole life's goal to get out. So you
can see how great I'm doing with my
life plan.

But to be honest—and I promised you that much—I guess I'd have to say that I have made it out of Slayton four times. Three times to rehab, once to the loony bin. Not exactly what I had in mind. The only thing I got out of the mental hospital was a line on some prescription meds that, for a while, worked almost as good as the white stuff I wouldn't want you to know about. I've been able to get the pills from Matt since I've been back, but they don't work like they used to.

Nothing does.

I'm writing you this letter from the bar where I work. It's slow today. My boss drove over to Polk to meet with some driver who promised him a deal on import beer. I told him nothing good's going to come out of Polk, but he doesn't listen to me. I'm just the cocktail waitress. Besides, the last time Boss Wells listened to a female was when he was crying in his crib.

Sorry about my handwriting. My hands shake if I drink, and they shake even more if I don't. I could use a computer at the library to write you, but it's not like they welcome me over there, not even before I dropped out of high school. So this is it, kid.

Tonight I'm going out with Ben again. Okay, not out. Just to my place or to his car. It doesn't matter. What matters is that for an hour with Ben, I won't feel. And when he gives me the pills he's bringing from Matt's,

I'll have the promise of not feeling more. That's all I ask. To get the gnawing inside of me to stop, even for an hour. A minute.

❊

The front door smacked open, then slammed shut. Maggie Dale shoved the letter into the pocket of her short, tight denim skirt.

"Maggie? You got it dark enough in this joint." Gary, one of the regulars, was okay as long as he didn't drink too much. He could be a mean drunk. Maggie had found that out the hard way. She wouldn't let it happen again.

"The Well is a bar, Gary. If you want bright, go to the tanning booth cross the street." The only light in the bar came from a row of fake Tiffany stained-glass lamps hanging from the ceiling. That, and the glow of the TV behind the counter.

Most customers seemed to like it dark. They settled on wooden stools that lined the mahogany bar, worn smooth by the weight of men's arms. Not Gary. He thought he owned the table closest to the door. Half a dozen tables were scattered across the uneven floor. Maggie served buffalo wings and cold sandwiches for those who wanted an excuse to drink longer. Night and day, the bar smelled of beer and bourbon.

One of Gary's buddies, a relative newcomer to town, stormed into the bar like thunder in a hurry. He nodded, then pulled up a seat at Gary's table. "Maggie, come over here and keep us company, girl! This place is dead empty."

Maggie liked the sound of the words *dead empty*. She

said them over again in her head and fingered the scar on her left wrist. She wore bracelets to hide the white ridge where the blade had slid as easily as if she'd been cutting a slice of lemon meringue. That had surprised her more than the fact that she'd slit her wrist for no good reason, other than the realization that there was no good reason not to. She hadn't even been able to come up with somebody to write a suicide note to.

Dead empty. That was how she'd felt when she'd taken the blade out of her razor and turned it around to get a good hold. They just didn't make razors like they used to, like they looked in the movies, when a beautiful woman slid into a bubbly bathtub and ended it all. Maggie had had to break her plastic razor to get at the blade. She'd gotten the sharp edge to cut deep enough to make her pass out, although the whiskey and pills may have had something to do with that.

When she'd come to on the floor of her dirty apartment kitchen, her first thought had been, *So I can't even do that right. . . .*

"Maggie?" Gary shouted, jerking her back to the present.

His buddy slapped his knee again. "You coming or not, darlin'?"

Most of Gary's buddies could be good tippers, even though Maggie wouldn't have wanted to be stuck in a grain elevator with any of them. "Hey, handsome," she countered, strutting to their table. "And just who's going to get you your beer if I'm over here on your lap?"

He laughed, his mouth open, showing one brown tooth. "Now that *is* a devil of a choice!"

Maggie took their orders and filled them. Her boss

still wasn't back, so she poured herself a shot of Jack Daniel's and carried all three drinks to the table. She drank hers standing up. It burned in her chest, and she waited for it to reach her head.

"You hold your liquor better than any girl I know, Maggie," Gary commented, as if he'd taught her everything she knew about it.

"Practice, practice, practice." Maggie forced a smile that would pay off when they left their tips. Some guys a whole lot nicer than Gary and his buddies could walk a check without padding so much as 10 percent, even if she did handstands.

Maggie could remember her first drink of hard liquor. At 10 years old, she'd already hated the smell of whiskey almost as much as what it made her daddy do when he drank it. He'd given her sips of beer before she could say the word *beer*. Those sips didn't count, though. Her first real drink had been an offering, something the old man had done after he'd hit her too much—gone so far he'd actually felt bad about it. She hadn't cried though, not even when the blood filled her mouth and trickled down her chin and onto her pajamas.

"You're a tough kid," he'd said, grabbing the whiskey bottle with a fist that looked skinned, the knuckles red and swollen. "You earned this."

He'd poured her a glass from a bottle so dark brown she'd expected that whatever came from it would feel like mud sliding down her throat. But it hadn't. She'd drunk it down like lemonade. Afterward, she'd coughed and choked, blood spurting out with the whiskey.

Her daddy had laughed as she doubled over. Her stomach had pinched together, making her feel like she'd vomit right there . . . something that would have gotten her another smack for sure. When she'd caught her breath again and made her eyes stop watering, she'd asked for another glass.

She'd been asking ever since.

He'd left home three years later, and Maggie had never heard from him again.

> "I want everybody to have a good life. That's why I came. That's why my Father sent me."

The words came from the TV above the bar. Maggie turned. A man was being interviewed on the steps of a Worship House in West Salem, Ohio. Laced canopy stretched over the lawn. Long tables with white tablecloths held empty casserole dishes and roast turkey carved to the bone. The man talking was average-looking, lean but strong, with clear green eyes that seemed to hold the interviewer captive. He was wearing a brown suit with a striped shirt. Maggie guessed he might have been in his early thirties.

"There's that guy again," Gary said. "Joshua." He shushed a group of men just coming into the bar. They were backslapping each other and laughing as if they'd already drunk their limit at some other bar.

Maggie knew who Joshua was. You'd have to be living in a cave not to have heard of him. She'd never met him or seen him in person, but a lot of people who came into the bar had.

He'd been in the news off and on, but she couldn't remember getting a good look at him on TV before now. They said he was camera shy, and as she watched him, she believed it. He nodded at the newscaster, then walked away.

The camera shifted to an anchorwoman inside the Worship House.

> "Here in the town of West Salem, Ohio, I'm talking with the mother of the bride. Tell us what went on here today."

She shoved the mike into the face of a middle-aged woman, wearing a mother-of-the-bride dress—coral satin. Something she'd never wear again, Maggie thought.

> "It was absolutely amazing!"

The woman scratched her head, as if she still couldn't make sense of it all, before she continued.

> "More people came to the reception than we expected, and we ran out of champagne before the wedding toast. I was so embarrassed. So I said something to my friend from Polk, Mary Davidson. She said something to her son Josh. They had a discussion, and then Josh went back with the waiters and—"

"Look! There's Pete!" Gary shouted. "He's all dressed up fit to kill." Gary pointed at the TV. "There's Andy!"

"Quiet!" Maggie demanded, pushing past them to get

a better view. She did see Pete and Andy, although she barely recognized them in their suits and ties. They were brothers, and they ran the auto-mechanics shop across the street. Pete played minor-league ball for the Toledo Mud Hens. Maggie had gone to school with them. She turned up the volume on the TV. The mother of the bride was still speaking.

"I know you're not going to believe this. But . . . well, there wasn't any champagne. I'll swear to that. And then there was champagne everywhere! Just like that! It gushed from that fountain over there. And it came out of the faucets, instead of water! It was the best champagne I've ever tasted. Everybody said so."

The anchorwoman turned to face the camera.

"Not exactly everybody. I've interviewed a number of guests who said that this wasn't the first champagne fountain they've seen at weddings here, even when Joshua wasn't present."

She stuck the mike in the face of a guy who looked like he'd had a few too many.

"What do you think of the champagne situation?"
"I'm a beer man."
"But what about the dramatic appearance of champagne? Would you call it a miracle?"

The guy shrugged.

Dandi Daley MacKall

"They ran out. How should I know where they got it?"

Maggie reached up and turned off the TV. "Well, we might as well close the bar. Free champagne? That Josh character will put us all out of business."

The men laughed with her. "How do you think he did it?" Gary asked. "Some kind of group hypnosis?"

Maggie went back to serving drinks, while speculation about Josh drifted around the room. She listened to the guys pool their ignorance, until she couldn't take it anymore. "Any of you ever seen him? Josh . . . what's his last name again?"

"Davidson." The answer came from a man Maggie was pretty sure she'd never seen before today. He'd come in with a group of guys and stayed on to nurse his second beer. A leather case sat at his feet, and a camera rested on the bar in front of him. He was well dressed and nice-looking—dark hair, good haircut, brown eyes, pale skin. He wore a polo shirt and gray pants. She smelled tobacco on him. Since she'd quit smoking—for the fifth time—she could pick up the scent a mile away.

"Do you know him? that Joshua guy?" She swiped at the bar with a rag.

The man shook his head and grinned. He had a nice smile. "Not really. I'm just trying to get his photograph. I've met him a couple of times. He's an interesting guy." He held out his hand to Maggie. "My name's Jude Smith."

Maggie wiped her hand on her skirt before she shook his. "Maggie Dale." She eyed the camera. It looked expensive, like Jude's shoes. She nodded at the camera. "You do this for a living?"

"I work for *The Query*."

Maggie had seen *Query* in supermarket checkout lines. Headlines ranged from "Aliens in School" to which movie star was dating which other movie star while married to another movie star. "Don't think I've ever met a paparazzi before," she joked.

She thought she saw a flash of anger, but it disappeared into a smile.

"Is that right?" Jude took a long sip of his beer. "I've met plenty of cocktail waitresses." He laughed, as if he was just kidding with her.

Maybe he was. Then he stood up, put down a 20 on the bar, and walked away, leaving her the biggest tip so far today.

Maggie waited until he was gone before tucking the money into her pocket, next to Chance's letter. She had no idea what to make of Jude Smith. But then, what else was new? Nobody had ever accused Maggie Dale of having great insight into men.

❖

After work, Maggie drove her old Ford Galaxy to her apartment. She never referred to the one-room, second-floor flat as "home," even though she'd lived there for almost a year. It was in a small complex of six apartments, a five-minute drive from work.

After she'd dropped out of high school less than a

Dandi Daley Mackall

month before graduation, she'd moved out of her mom's house. The only place she could afford to rent had been the room above the bar. She'd been too young to serve drinks, but Boss Wells had paid her to sweep the place and do odd jobs. She'd worked nights bagging groceries six days a week at the Slayton Market. When she turned 21, Boss Wells hired her on full-time at the bar. She'd moved into her own apartment the day before her twenty-first birthday.

Maggie climbed the back stairs, holding her breath until she was well past the first landing, where the stench of uncollected and rotting garbage drew a cloud of gnats. She unlocked her door and flipped on the light.

The apartment smelled like musty carpet and old pennies. The furniture had come with the apartment, and Maggie hadn't bothered changing it—brown couch, blue recliner, a table, and two chairs.

Everywhere she looked, there were "sad spots." That's how she thought of them. The corner where she'd slid to the floor and cried the day she'd moved in. The spot where Alan had stood when he'd called her a slut, his voice calm and controlled, on the last night she'd seen him. The kitchen sink, where she'd watched the blood from her wrist mingle with ice water and spin pink down the drain.

She grabbed a yogurt from the fridge, curled up on the couch, and clicked the remote control. They were talking about Joshua again. FOX News had picked up the story about the wedding champagne. But again Josh had declined to be interviewed.

"Honestly," she muttered. The news wasn't much more

reliable than *The Query* these days. She changed channels. ABC had a roundtable discussion. Normally, she couldn't care less about politics, but it was funny to see politicians fight over Joshua. The red states claimed Joshua was on their side. He supported the Ten Commandments, opposed abortion, reaffirmed trust in God, advocated reading the Scriptures and adhering to moral codes. But the blue states claimed Joshua as a strong proponent of peace and nonviolence, a champion of the poor and underprivileged.

There was a knock at the door.

Maggie checked the clock: 11:30. Ben was right on time. She'd been seeing him for two months. In the beginning, she'd actually thought they might have something together. He was quite a bit older than she was, with a good job in Rocky River. Although he swore he wasn't married, she'd never been to his house. It made her wonder.

He knocked again.

She turned off the TV and answered the door. Ben came in and took her in his arms. Maggie closed her eyes and kissed him, trying to block out everything from her mind and get back the feelings she'd had for him in the beginning. He'd swept her off her feet then, and she'd thought about him all the time, counting the hours until they'd see each other again.

On their third "date," Ben had pulled some weed from his glove compartment, and a revolver had tumbled out. Ben had laughed it off and said he needed it for protection after work. Maggie had laughed with him, but she hadn't been able to get the gun out of her head.

Now, as they kissed and his hands roved up and down

Dandi Daley Mackall

her body, all she thought of was the gun. If Ben couldn't fill her mind anymore, if he could no longer take her thoughts away from the gnawing of total emptiness, then maybe his gun could.

Chapter Two

Ben took what he wanted from her, and Maggie did the same. She thought about the gun the whole time and despised herself for being too much of a coward to use it. She'd always been a coward. Lack of courage had defined her life. Why should her death be any different?

When they were done, neither of them had much to say. Maggie turned on the lamp. "What did you bring?"

The gnawing that had almost disappeared for all of a minute and a half was back now, more intense. As if the beast inside her had only left long enough to get his buddies and bring them back.

"Come on, Benny." She played with the blond hair that fell over his forehead. She willed her eyes to look soft, inviting . . . not desperate. "You brought your little Maggie something, didn't you?"

Ben dug in his pants pockets and came out with a white packet. He shook out a few purple pills. "Don't take more than two, Maggie. I mean it."

They each took two, without water, and waited. She leaned back on the pillow, impatient for whatever lived inside the pills to take possession of her. She wanted that, needed something to take herself off her hands, if only for a night.

Ben lit a cigarette and leaned against the rough headboard. Maggie hated the stench of cigarette smoke, but she didn't say anything. Ben knew she hated it, especially in her apartment. He blew out a gray cloud that seemed to come from deep inside him. "I'm going to have to line up somebody new. Maybe out of Polk."

"What do you mean?" Maggie asked. The pills were starting to work. She could feel the cat claws inside her chest loosen. Sounds were clear but muffled, as if she were a kid in a wool scarf, bundled up to play in the snow.

Ben coughed. His chest rattled with it. "Matt's not dealing anymore."

Maggie sat up straight. "Matt? *Our* Matt's not dealing? You're kidding."

"Nope. Word's out. He's finished with the whole scene."

Maggie knew Matt didn't use. Good dealers didn't. But he'd been a dealer since she'd known him in junior high.

He'd made a fortune in the business and had never been caught, not even once. She couldn't believe he'd quit. He wasn't the type. What else would he do?

She didn't want to think about it. She didn't want to think about anything. Maggie closed her eyes and let the pills take her wherever they would.

❊

When she opened her eyes, it was still dark and Ben was gone. She didn't miss him, not like she would have a month ago. But a vague loneliness swallowed her whole, like a python gulping down its prey.

She turned the bedside clock around and saw that she'd been sleeping three hours. The pills had worn off. She punched Ben's pillow, angry with herself for wasting drug time sleeping. Now she was awake and felt worse than before, like someone had wound her insides as tight as they'd go and at any moment might choose to let it all fly loose. She could come unwound. Then what?

She reached for the envelope on the night table and peeked inside. Ben had left her five pills. She knew he wasn't in love with her any more than she was in love with him. But at least he treated her decent. If she took one pill every day, she'd be good until she saw him again on Wednesday.

She dropped the envelope into the drawer and slammed it shut. The bang echoed in the barren room. Outside, gravel crunched as a truck bounced down her street. Scratchy TV voices came from the apartment below. The old couple who lived in 1C with their scrawny cat left the

TV on all night every night. Maggie pulled the pillow over her ears and squeezed her eyes shut.

It was no use. Her skin felt sticky, and the room smelled like paint, as it did whenever the humidity got this thick. She put on her robe and pushed open a window. The sky—at least what she could see of it between apartment buildings—looked gray-black and starless.

Maggie sat on the bed and opened the night-table drawer. She could take one pill now. Then she wouldn't have one to take tomorrow. Shoot, it *was* tomorrow. She tried to shake out one pill, but two fell into her palm. She took them both because taking one was a waste.

The room smoothed out, the corner edges fading into walls and swooping to the floor. Even when she closed her eyes, the walls moved. She thought she was going to be sick, but it passed. Everything passed.

Thunder crashed. Maggie felt the bed shake. Her heart twitched. The white curtains billowed into the room. She ran to the window just as thunder struck again. A streak of lightning speared the earth. Her hands shook as she lowered and locked the window. The smell of wet leaves and dust-turned-mud brought back a time when she used to love storms. That was a long time ago. She hated them now. It was ridiculous, but the panic was there, as if the house were on fire and she couldn't get out.

She took two more pills and waited for dawn. At 5 a.m. Maggie sat curled in her chair, her knees drawn up. There was still no light, but the thunder had stopped, and the rain died down to a sprinkle. She took the last pill and waited.

Nothing. It didn't do a thing, except make her head

pound and her ears buzz. She added two aspirin and dragged herself to the shower.

When she came out, she dialed 9 on her cell. It wasn't very bright to have your dealer on speed-dial, but Maggie figured she hadn't been very bright for years. Why start now?

The phone rang once. Twice. Three times.

Matt answered on the fourth ring. "Yeah?"

"Matt, sorry. Did I wake you?"

She heard a yawn. "Nah. I should be getting up. How are you, Maggie?"

"Getting up? This is your going-to-bed time." She laughed, but it sounded fake, even to her. "I've been hearing some nasty rumors about you."

"What?"

"Ben was by. He said you're getting out of the business."

"He's right."

"Come on! What's with that?"

"I'm starting over." He sounded different in a way she couldn't put her finger on.

"Okay. Whatever. But I need you, Matt. I'm coming by this morning, okay?"

"Can't do it, Maggie."

She kept her voice light, teasing. They'd known each other a long time. They'd been in the same class in high school. Matt graduated the year she should have. "For me? Please? I have to be your oldest customer. Eighth grade, remember?"

He was quiet for a minute. When he spoke, it was like there was pain behind each word. "I'm sorry about that, Maggie. I'm sorry about a lot of things, including everything

I did to you. You don't know how much I wish I could go back and undo everything. I could make excuses for dealing, but there aren't any. It was wrong, and I knew it was wrong."

"Hey! Lighten up, guy. I'm just joking around with you."

"I know."

She was pacing now. She crossed to the kitchen and opened the fridge. Leftover pizza, a carton of Chinese take-out, one yogurt, a bag of coffee, a bottle of beer, and a can of Coke. She needed coffee, but she didn't have cream for it. She hated coffee without cream. Maggie slammed the fridge door. "You have to have something left—just to tide me over until I can make other arrangements?"

"No, Maggie."

"You're serious, aren't you?"

"Yep."

"Well, that's just great." Her anger sparked, then burned deep into her, seeping into muscles and tendons. She'd relied on Matt's connections since she was 14. He owed her. "Who's taking over?" She knew Matt had kept the prices down as much as he could for her, for old time's sake. Somebody new, that could cost. "Where do I go? Give me a number."

"You need to quit, Maggie. I wish I knew what to say to you that would—"

"You're not my shrink!" she snapped. "Or my parole officer. You're my dealer."

"I'm your friend. And I'm not your dealer anymore— or anyone else's."

If he *were* her friend, then he'd know how she was feel-ing right now. She *needed* him. She needed what he could

Dandi Daley Mackall

give her. "What happened to you, Matt? Is somebody pushing you out?"

He got quiet again. Then he sighed heavily into the phone. "I met Joshua."

Maggie was stunned. She didn't know which was crazier—Matt meeting Joshua, or Joshua meeting Matt the Drug Dealer.

"You know who I'm talking about, right? Joshua Davidson, from Polk?"

"No way! What did he do? Turn your drugs into powdered sugar?"

Matt laughed. "You heard about the water-to-champagne thing too, huh? I can't wait to talk to Pete. He and Andy were there."

Maggie waited, trying to imagine how Matt and Joshua could have ended up in the same place. Or Pete and Andy, for that matter, even though they went to a Worship House, or at least they'd gone when they were in high school. Matt probably had never seen the inside of a Worship House or a Community Hall. And those were the only two choices if somebody wanted to go and get *religious*.

"So how did you meet him?" she asked.

"I was doing what I do every night, hanging in East Cleveland, dealing to my boys. And Joshua walked by. He had Pete and Andy with him, and a couple other guys we knew in high school. Josh stopped. Then he just started talking to us. He talked about God. He called God his Father. But there was something about him . . . about Josh, I mean. You think I sound crazy, huh?"

"Like Crazy John," Maggie muttered. She felt bad after

she'd said it. Crazy John was what they called the homeless guy who stood on street corners and yelled at people that they'd better repent or else.

Matt went right back to telling his story. "So I was leaning against my new wheels, making a sale, while Josh was talking to some of the boys. He talked to everybody. And I mean *everybody*—prostitutes, dealers, junkies, gangs. I watched him, Maggie, the way he was with everybody. Like they counted. The kids down there loved him, and you know they hate everybody outside.

"Then Joshua turned to me and smiled. Right at me. It felt like he could see straight through me, past everything I'd ever done in my whole life. Like he was sticking a knife inside and carving out every bad thing I ever did. Then he said, 'Matt, come on.'"

"Come on?" Maggie repeated.

"Something like that. He called me by my name— I figured Andy had been talking to him about me—and he asked me to come with him. I can't remember the words exactly, but I knew what he meant. He meant I should leave everything, including the shipment I'd just got in, prime stuff I'd paid a bundle for—the chance to make more money than I've ever seen in one place. He wanted me to leave it all to go with him."

Maggie wanted to demand where Matt had left this shipment, this "prime stuff." But she let him talk.

"I didn't even think about it, Maggie. I opened my case and poured everything down the sewer we were standing over." He laughed. "My boys tried to stop me, but they were too late. I thought they were going to off me."

"No wonder."

"I've flushed everything. And I'm emptying my bank accounts to build a youth center in Cleveland, where I've been dealing all these years. I want to try to make a difference with the kids there."

Maggie did not want to talk about kids in Cleveland or anywhere else. She'd heard enough. She wasn't going to get a thing out of Matt. She could see that. "Well, call me when you change your mind." She started to hang up.

"Wait, Maggie! Don't hang up!"

She put the phone back to her ear but didn't say anything. Unless he'd changed his mind already, she wasn't interested in anything Matt had to say.

"I'm having a party," he said.

She relaxed. "Well, now you're talking." Over the years, Matt had put on some of the best parties Maggie had ever been to. That's where she had met Ben, in fact. Matt would bring out whatever new thing hit the street. He'd been the first person she knew to supply methamphetamines.

"Not *that* kind of party, Maggie. More like a dinner. I want you to come. I could use your help."

Maggie figured that even if Matt kept this up and refused to deal, somebody at his party would be ready and willing. "Sure. When?"

"Day after tomorrow. My place. Bring anybody you want. Bring Ben if you want to."

She'd think about it.

Right now Maggie had much more important things on her mind. Like getting through the day.

Chapter Three

Maggie pulled on jeans and a T-shirt and checked her purse for cash. Last night had been a good night for tips. She thought about the photographer or journalist, or whatever he was, and wondered if he ever got his picture of Joshua Davidson.

She had plenty of time to drive to Cleveland and back before her shift at the bar. Morning wasn't the best time to make connections, but if she drove up and down 135th and over to Kinsman, she could probably find somebody who was dealing. She didn't like to do it this way, but Matt hadn't left her much choice.

The back stairs to the gravel parking lot were so wet that Maggie had to hang on to the iron railing to keep from slipping. Her Ford beater fit right in with the other cars, none of them parked straight, as if they'd dropped from the sky with the raindrops.

She caught a glimpse of herself in the rearview as she climbed behind the wheel. As hard as she tried to distance herself from her mother, there she was in that mirror, looking back at her. Maggie had her mother's big green eyes, prominent forehead, skin taut over high cheekbones. And they both had dark, out-of-control, curly hair. At least her mother used to. Maggie hadn't seen her in over a year.

The safety-belt reminder bell kept up a steady *ding, ding, ding.* But it felt too hypocritical to fasten her seat belt, when the scars from cutting her own wrists were still soft and fleshy. Even she had some standards.

She turned the key. The engine growled, then stopped. Maggie pumped the pedal and tried again. It caught on the third try. The Ford had been on its last legs since the day she bought it. If it hadn't been for Andy at the auto repair, the car would have been scrap metal by now.

Before Maggie even reached the highway, the Ford stalled out twice. She slapped the steering wheel. She was never going to make it to Cleveland. Who was she kidding? And if she stalled down on 105th, then what?

She made a sharp U-turn and headed back to town, letting the Ford coast downhill. She rolled past the Sons of

Dandi Daley Mackall

Thunder Motorcycles lot. Maggie knew the owner's sons, Bob and Brad. She and Brad had been in the same class at school, and the brothers had worked in their dad's shop even back then. Andy had worked with them for a while as a mechanic before opening his own garage.

Maggie's brakes squealed as she pulled into Andy's, under the big sign that read Mud Hens Garage. Andy's brother, Pete, was an ace pitcher for the Toledo Mud Hens. Having somebody on a triple-A minor-league team was a big deal for a town the size of Slayton. Maggie doubted the boys' auto-repair business would have made it if it hadn't been for Pete's semicelebrity status around town.

She coaxed the car to the top of the gravel drive. The Ford rattled, then shut off on its own, as if it didn't need Maggie to tell it what to do.

Andy was just inside the open garage, bent over a white beater pickup. The truck's engine lay on the ground beside him. He looked up and smiled at Maggie, showing the whitest teeth.

She could still remember the time in fourth grade when Andy had stuck up for her and made a group of fifth-grade boys leave her alone. Andy had been thin then, and he was still thin and wiry, with curly black hair. His big brother, Pete, had gotten all the attention in high school as a star athlete, but Andy never seemed to mind. He never seemed to mind anything. Maggie remembered him reading his Scriptures during lunch, smiling good-naturedly when kids teased him about it.

He walked out to meet her. "Hey, Maggie! How are you?"

Desperately lonely. In dire need of a hit. Semisuicidal. Dead empty. "Fine," she answered.

Andy shook his head at the Ford. "Car trouble again, huh?"

"I always knew you were a prophet, Andy. Can you fix it? Fast?" If he could do it in the next hour, she could still get to Cleveland and make a buy. Already her arms felt as if termites were eating their way through her skin. She rubbed her forearms.

Andy pulled a wrench out of his back pocket and moved to examine the car as Maggie got out. "I'll do my best. But I'm guessing we'll have to find a part or two. That's going to take a couple of days anyway. I'll give you top priority, though, okay? Lucky for you, Pete's been a little off his pitching game. When he's hot, we're so busy around here I can't even breathe."

Panic gripped Maggie's chest. Without a car, it would be hard to get to Cleveland and buy what she needed. It took everything she had to hide her reaction from Andy. "So people don't give you business if Pete's not hot?" She scratched her arms, then made herself stop.

Andy had his head under the hood of the Ford. "When Pete's pitching great, guys get their cars fixed here, even when they don't need it. I don't really get it either. Pete's hardly ever in the shop, so they don't see him. I suppose saying that they got their cars fixed in Pete's shop is the next best thing. People are funny that way."

Funny was the last thing Maggie was feeling.

A radio was on in the garage, the volume up loud

enough to hear crowd noise and an excited announcer screaming, *"It's out of here! A home run!"*

Andy stood up so fast that he bumped his head on the raised hood. "Pete." He sighed. "Second home run Pete's given up this afternoon."

Maggie made herself respond as if her insides weren't being gnawed on. She was usually better at hiding her cravings. She swallowed and willed her voice to sound normal. "Pete's not doing so well then?"

"I don't know. I think he's in a little slump. He'll get out of it, though."

Maggie and everybody else had expected Pete to be in the majors by now, breaking all kinds of pitching *and* batting records. But Andy had always been his brother's number one fan.

He went back to work under the hood. "Hey, have you seen John lately?"

"Crazy John?" Maggie asked. "Now that you mention it, no. I haven't seen him for a while. Aren't you two still buddies?"

"John's not crazy, you know."

"So you've told me."

Sometimes John hung out in front of Maggie's bar, trying to convince people to stop sinning and "turn to God." He made Maggie nervous. Not because he dressed weird, but because when he looked at her, she got the feeling that he knew her ugliest, deepest, darkest secrets.

"I haven't seen him for a couple days. He's probably out in the woods somewhere by himself. He goes off to pray." Andy took a greasy rag out of his pocket and used it to turn the radiator cap. Water spit up. "I guess I haven't seen that much of John since I've been working with Josh."

"Is everybody hopping on Joshua's bandwagon? Almost makes me feel sorry for poor John."

Andy grinned. "John was the one who introduced me to Josh. He's been trying to get all of us to follow Joshua, instead of him. John says the whole reason he's on earth is to get people ready to follow Josh."

"You're kidding." That wasn't something any man Maggie had ever known would say.

"You should come to Worship House sometime," Andy suggested. "Listen to Joshua talk or hear him read from the Scriptures. It's like he wrote them himself."

It had been a long time since Maggie's parents had dragged her to Worship House. In town, most of the people attended services either at a Worship House or at the Community Hall, if they considered themselves more "liberal minded." Maggie had no use for either group. She believed all the important people in town attended so they could look down on everyone who didn't.

She changed the subject. "I saw you on TV, Andy."

"Me?"

"At that wedding in West Salem. You looked good all dressed up. What really went on down there anyway?"

Andy looked at her, his wrench suspended as if he were about to conduct an orchestra but couldn't remember the song. "That was a miracle." He said it quietly, without a hint of irony . . . or doubt.

"A miracle?" She heard the ridicule in her voice and didn't bother covering it.

Andy didn't react. "Maggie, remember how we used to talk in study hall about God promising to send his Son to us?"

Maggie laughed, remembering. "*You* did all the talking, as I recall. And I always told you the 'son' was probably going to be a 'daughter' because she was waiting so long to make an entrance." She'd given Andy a hard time, but she'd liked the idea of someone coming to save the world. Even before her fateful senior year, she'd dreamed about someone who would come and save her. Instead the only one who'd shown up was Alan, and "saving" her never entered his mind.

Andy's gaze was steady on her. "It's Joshua, Maggie."

He was perfectly serious. She could see that.

"Is that what he told you?" She felt protective of Andy. He was so good-hearted, so gullible.

"It's true, Maggie. Joshua Davidson is the Son of God we've been waiting for." He smiled at her, then ducked under the hood of her car.

Claws dug into her stomach again. "I better get to work, Andy."

She left her car with him and sprinted across the blacktop road to the bar. She needed something to settle her down. She didn't have to be at work for another hour. If the boss hadn't come in yet, she could get herself a drink. Just one. To get her started.

She was almost to the front door when Crazy John stepped out of the shadows. He wore sandals, old cutoffs, and a T-shirt that had seen better days. Long, tangled hair hung over leathery, brown skin. His eyebrows were as thick as hairy fingers.

"Hi, John." She brushed past him to unlock the door. "Andy and I were just talking about you. Where've you been?" She dropped the keys, and he picked them up and handed them to her.

"God loves you, Maggie." He spoke in a Darth Vader voice, deep and too loud. "God knows everything about you. You can't fool him. He sees everything. You need to agree with him, admit that what you've done, what you're doing, is wrong and separates you from God and all that's holy—"

She fumbled with the keys. Maybe he said the same thing to everybody because the words were one-size-fits-all. Like Chinese fortune cookies. But whenever he spoke to her, Maggie felt naked, exposed, and filthy. She wanted to get inside the bar and away from him. The lock finally gave, and she tugged the door open.

"Get ready for Joshua, Maggie!" John called after her. "Confess your sins!"

She forced herself to turn back and smile casually at him. "That would take too much of God's time, John." Then she slipped inside the bar and closed the door after her.

Maggie took advantage of the empty bar to pour herself a glass of gin. She didn't much care for the taste of gin, but you couldn't smell it on your breath like you could whiskey or scotch. She downed a second glass. It wasn't enough, but it dulled her edges. She hid the bottle behind the others and rinsed out her glass.

The empty bar should have been quiet, but Maggie found it noisier when she was here alone than when it was filled with brawlers and bikers. The floor creaked. She

Dandi Daley Mackall

thought she heard a mouse or a squirrel pacing inside the north wall. The cooler buzzed.

She sat at the back table and took out her paper and pencil.

Dear Chance,

I miss you. Do you believe me? I hope you do. I never imagined I would—or could—miss you like this. I thought I could forget all about you. Wish I'd known. Wish somebody would have told me this part.

If you were here, it would be an ordinary day. I wouldn't be using. We'd get Andy to take us to one of Pete's games, and you could sit in the dugout. We might even have the kind of life where people invite us to weddings and turn water into champagne. I can see your eyes growing big as you try to figure out how Joshua did that.

We might drive out to the farm so I could show you where I grew up.

Maggie put away her letter because that last part was a lie, and she'd promised not to lie to Chance. He wouldn't be any more welcome at her mother's home than she was herself.

About a year ago, when Maggie had been coming out of the Laundromat, she'd spotted her mother across the highway. Maggie had dropped her basket of clean clothes, not caring when they rolled in the dirt and blew through the grass. She'd run across the highway without looking.

Cars honked. Tires squealed.

Maggie had screamed, "Mom! Mom!"

Before she could reach her mother, she'd seen those cold, green eyes turn toward her. Her mother's hatred was as fresh as the day she'd figured out why her daughter had been vomiting every morning before the school bus came. Maggie had stood motionless on the curb and watched her mom climb into a van and drive off.

"Maggie, what are you doing here?" Her boss had come through the back and surprised her. No small trick, since he weighed close to 300 pounds and had never been light on his size-13 feet.

Maggie felt in her pocket to make sure the letter was there. As soon as she could, she'd move it to her backpack with her other letters to Chance. "My car broke down."

"Again? When are you going to get a decent car?"

"When you give me a decent raise. Andy can fix it. He's working on it now."

"You better hope he's a better mechanic than his brother is a baseball player. The Mud Hens are losing again." Maggie's boss was the kind of fan who loved Pete when he was winning and hated him when he wasn't. "They pulled Pete after four innings. He better get his act together. Turn on the game and see if we can get the final score."

Maggie walked behind the bar and reached up to turn on the TV.

"Aw, great!" Boss stared out the front window. "When did Crazy John get back? I'm calling the cops again if he scares off a single customer."

"He's not hurting anybody," Maggie observed.

"Since when did you and Crazy John get so chummy?"

She let that one go. Boss Wells didn't like anybody disagreeing with him, and Maggie needed this job. She knew that she brought in more repeat business than his watered-down scotch, but life and jobs never came with guarantees.

The day dragged on. Customers blended into one another. They made the same small talk with her, told the same jokes, ordered the same drinks. She was able to sneak in a couple shots over lunch, when the boss went home.

After work, she picked up a pizza from Vinny's and a bottle of cheap wine from the liquor store and walked them both home. The walk took her 30 minutes, and by the time she got home, she'd lost her appetite.

But not her thirst. She finished the bottle and passed out on the couch. Her last conscious thought was, *One less day to live through.*

Chapter Four

The next day Maggie talked her boss into letting her off early. She kept herself going by thinking about Matt's party and sneaking shots whenever she could. Maggie couldn't imagine a party at Matt's without drugs everywhere. Coke and heroin flowing freely. Vicodin, OxyContin, Stadol, Percodan—all kinds of pills set out in colorful bowls like candy. But even if Matt had been serious about no drugs, there would be other dealers at the party.

Ben came by the bar for her at

a quarter past seven, fifteen minutes late. She put on lipstick without looking, ran her fingers through her hair, and told her boss she was leaving. She and Ben didn't kiss hello or hold hands as they walked out. They were past that.

"Mind if I stop at Andy's and see if my car's ready yet?" she asked, already crossing the street toward the shop.

Ben shrugged and lit a cigarette.

When she got closer to the garage, Maggie saw the Closed sign on the door. "Great. Are the Mud Hens playing tonight?"

"I don't think so," Ben answered. "Let's get going."

Maggie followed Ben to his car. "I'm out of pills, Ben." She got in Ben's side and slid over, hoping Ben was in a good mood.

Make that a *generous* mood.

"I'm out, too, Maggie. I don't even have weed." He took a long drag on his cigarette, then tossed it out the window and immediately lit another. Maggie thought his hands were shaking.

They didn't chat as he drove, too fast, into Cleveland. Maggie stared at Ben's glove compartment. She could see the gun in her mind's eye, as if she were Superman with X-ray vision. She knew it had to be there, only inches from her. She wondered if Ben kept it loaded. He probably did. Ben was a loaded-gun kind of guy. Maggie liked the thought of the gun there within her reach. Like a safety net, a back door. A lifeline.

Ben took the Parma exit, just south of Cleveland. "I'll ask around tonight. I'm thinking Lenny or maybe that bald guy we met at the last party can line us up." His fingers drummed the steering wheel.

Dozens of cars were parked in Matt's circular drive, on the street in front of his mansion, and all over the lawn. He'd moved into this multimillion-dollar house a year ago. Last month he'd shown Maggie his six-car garage out back, with a car in every spot.

Ben and she got out and walked toward the house. Through the lighted front windows Maggie saw long tables piled with food. Some people were sitting at the tables, while others walked around. She was so caught up looking in that she almost tripped over a big For Sale sign on the lawn. Ben didn't go out of his way to help her. She frowned at the sign, which looked new. "Is Matt selling his house?"

Ben shrugged and lit up again. It took him four flicks of his lighter to get it. They weaved through Mercedes, Caddies, BMWs, and little foreign cars Maggie didn't know the names of. Mixed in with the expensive cars were a few beaters, including an old white pickup that looked like the one she'd seen Andy working on.

Laughter streamed from the open door of the mansion as they walked up the stone steps, past white columns, and into the crowded entry. The aroma of beef and cooked apples met them at the door.

"Are we eating dinner here?" Ben asked, making it clear that this wasn't at all what he'd come for.

"I told you what Matt said," Maggie whispered. She saw Matt coming toward them and waved.

Ben's cigarette had grown a long, ashy tip, and he

reached for an ashtray on the closest end table. "Yeah, but I didn't think he—"

"You made it!" Matt strode up to them and hugged Maggie. There was something different about him, but she wouldn't have known how to describe it. He shook Ben's hand. "Cool! I didn't know if you guys would come or not."

"Always up for one of your parties, Matt," Ben said, a note of challenge, or at least irritability, in his voice.

Maggie knew she was staring at Matt, but she couldn't help it. There was something in his eyes, in the lines of his face, in the set of his shoulders. Happiness? Maybe that was it. She guessed she hadn't seen it often enough to know for sure. But that's what it looked like.

Matt grinned. "There's somebody I want you both to meet."

Ben glanced around the packed entry. People filled the living room and overflowed into the hallways. They stood and sat on the wide, open staircase leading to the second floor. They hung over the railings on the second and third floors.

"I don't know half these people, Matt," Ben complained. "And I need something. *Now*, man." Ben's jaw jerked sideways, a nervous twitch Maggie had seen a couple of times before. She was starting to think that Ben was in worse shape than she was.

"It's not that kind of party, Ben," Matt said. "I told Maggie—"

"I don't care what you told Maggie!" Ben snapped.

In the old days, that would have been enough for Matt

Dandi Daley Mackall

to have Ben thrown out. Matt was six-feet-four and 250 pounds of muscle and street smarts.

But instead of reacting, Matt put his hand on Ben's shoulder. "You'll be okay, Ben. Just hang on. You'll see. Why don't you find a seat and get something to eat?"

Ben shook off Matt's hand and waved at somebody at the other end of the room. "Hey, Lenny! Hey, man!" He turned his back on Maggie and Matt and shoved his way through the sea of guests.

Matt linked his arm through Maggie's. "Come on. I want you to meet Josh."

She followed him to the kitchen, which was almost as crowded as the living room. Maggie recognized a couple of girls from her old high school. Krystal was surrounded by men, as always. She didn't look a day older either, with shoulder-length black hair and a perfect figure. *Perky.* That's how Maggie had always summed up Krystal the Cheerleader. On a good day Maggie had just been ignored by Krystal and her friends. On a bad day, they'd mocked her or worse. Of the "Top Ten People Maggie Dale Would Hate to See at a Reunion," perky Krystal was right up there. The man next to her, the hottest guy in the room, put his arm around her waist, and she leaned into him, laughing.

"That's Michael Barnes," Matt informed her. "He owns the largest computer-software company this side of California. He and Krystal have been married about a year, I think."

Figures, Maggie thought. *The rich get richer, and the poor get poorer.*

Maggie turned her back on Krystal, who probably wouldn't have known who she was anyway, and spotted Andy peeling potatoes. "Andy! What are you doing here?"

"Hey, Maggie!" He grinned at her, then kept peeling. "Matt invited us. Pete's in the next room. Listen—I'm hoping to get that part in tomorrow so I can finish your car for you."

"That would rock, Andy."

The man next to Andy scooped the potato peels into a large trash bag that looked full, then headed outside with it. Maggie thought she'd seen him somewhere before, but she couldn't place him.

"That's who I want you to meet, Maggie," Matt said, pointing to the man with the trash bag. "That's Joshua."

Maggie watched the man lug the trash through the door. His arms were huge, but the rest of him was lean and unremarkable. Yet for a second, Maggie couldn't breathe. Maybe it was her crying need for something to take the edge off her nerves, but her heart pounded at panic speed. She wanted to leave, to get out of here now. She couldn't explain it. All she knew was that she did not want to meet the man they called Joshua.

"Maybe later, Matt. I better go find Ben." She backed away and bumped into someone.

"Sorry!" the woman said.

Maggie recognized her from high school. *Jessica something.*

"Maggie?" The woman smiled and squeezed Maggie's arm. "How *are* you? I'm so glad to see you!" She was still pretty, though not in Krystal's way. She'd gained a little

Dandi Daley Mackall

weight, and her bright red hair was shorter now. Jessica had been a good student, on the student council, the whole bit. She'd been decent to Maggie, even though she was three years older and light-years up the social-class structure. Maggie had heard that Jessica married Senator Sanders and moved to Washington. The papers called her a "trophy wife."

"Maggie, you remember Jessica," Matt said. "She's Jessica Sanders now."

Maggie nodded.

"Did the senator come with you, Jessica?" Matt asked.

Her smile faded. "Bob doesn't know I'm here, Matt. He . . . he doesn't approve."

"I'm sorry. I didn't know."

Maggie saw Josh heading toward them. "Nice to see you, Jessica." Slipping away through the crowd, she bypassed the living room and took the stairs to the second floor, stepping over people in private, intense conversations. On the landing, a crowd was gathered around somebody whose back was turned to her. It took Maggie a second to realize it was Pete. She stepped around the crowd and wandered through the upstairs rooms. This time she found no bowls of pills on the tables, no packets on the dressers, no boxes or syringes. Nothing. Not even in the den.

Maggie's throat was dry and her stomach queasy. Could she possibly get through the entire night without help? Could Ben? She didn't even see beer on the tables.

Someone came up behind her. "Maggie?"

It was Pete. He'd grown sideburns since the last time she'd seen him, and he'd filled out. He was well over six feet tall, with deep-set eyes and a broad nose.

"Well, if it isn't the famous baseball player!" She punched him playfully on the arm. It was rock solid.

"Guess you still don't follow the game, huh, Maggie? I haven't been very famous lately." He nodded toward the landing. "Every guy out there has pitching advice for me." He grinned at her. "I'm glad you made it. Matt said he'd invited you."

Matt and Pete had been mortal enemies in high school. Maggie wondered what had happened to change that.

Brad wandered in. He and his brother helped their dad run Sons of Thunder, a motorcycle and chop shop. People called the boys "Sons of Thunder," either because of the shop or because they could be pretty loud when they wanted to. In high school, the two sets of brothers—Pete and Andy, and Brad and Bob—had all hung out together. Maggie, an only child, had envied them. She still did.

"Maggie?" Brad walked up and shook her hand. "You look great! How've you been?"

"Thanks, Brad. Good. How about you? Are you still writing? Or does the cycle business keep you too busy?" Maggie could picture Brad writing in his journal on the bumpy school bus. He had written all the time, even during lunch. She and Brad had had a couple of English classes together, and Brad had always been the smartest in the class. Maggie used to love listening to his poetry in English lit. She'd expected that Brad would end up being a famous writer.

Brad smiled at her. "I'm still writing. Did you know Bob and I have been traveling with Joshua, helping out when we can?"

"You're kidding." First Pete and Andy. Then Matt. Now Brad and Bob? "I saw this lug on TV with Joshua the other day." She motioned toward Pete.

"You mean the wedding in West Salem?" Brad shook his head slowly. "I was there too. Pretty amazing, wasn't it?"

Amazing or not, Maggie had heard enough about it to last a lifetime. She needed to find Ben, or find Lenny, or find somebody who could give her what she needed. "So," she began, moving toward the door, "think we can get something to eat around here?"

"Not me," Pete answered, plopping onto the couch, the same couch Maggie had sat on half a dozen times to sample Matt's wares. "I'm going to hide out in here for a while. There's only so much baseball advice a man can take from guys who haven't played the game since elementary school."

Brad took Maggie's arm and led her toward the door. "Come on, Maggie. We'll leave this guy in peace."

She found Ben downstairs, and she and Brad sat down at a table across from him. Maggie could tell right away that Ben had scored. The furrows of his brow had dissolved. His eyes had a soft, pasty look to them. And he couldn't stop smiling. She wanted to leap across the table and slap his face for not finding her and sharing. Her only hope was that he'd bought extras. She'd have to hold on until then.

Some of the guests had already finished their salads. There was nothing to drink but water. Ben joked that Joshua ought to do that water-to-champagne trick of his. Maggie looked around for a head table, but there wasn't one. Then she saw Josh at one of the back tables, sitting between two women who had to be prostitutes. One wore a flesh-colored, net evening gown, and the other a black sequined top with a leather skirt.

The man at the head of Maggie's table stood up so suddenly, his water glass spilled. Brad tried to soak up the mess with his napkin. The man looked out of place in his expensive suit. His eyes were hard, the color and size of bullets. His manicured hands opened and closed into fists.

"This is ridiculous!" He spat out the words to the woman next to him. In her elegant black evening gown, she was as out of place as he was. "I wanted to hear Joshua speak, but look around! *This* is his audience? These drug dealers, criminals, prostitutes, and who knows what else? Some prophet this Joshua turned out to be! If he had any idea who was sitting at the same table with him right now, he'd bolt. Come on. We're getting out of here."

The man and woman stormed out of the room. Maggie turned to Josh's table. He was gazing after the couple. She thought he looked sad, but she knew he couldn't have heard what the man said—not from clear across the noisy room.

When Josh got up, the room quieted. "Healthy people don't need a doctor, do they?" He scanned the room, but Maggie had the feeling that he saw her. That he was talking to *her.* "I'm here for people whose lives are messed up, broken."

He glanced at the door, where the well-dressed couple were putting on jackets. "This is exactly where I want to be, with people who know they're sinning, not with people who think they're good enough already." Josh's smile filled the room, and so did his voice, although he hadn't raised it. "Are you thankful to my Father in heaven for this food Matt has had prepared for us? Then let's enjoy it and be grateful!"

They ate an amazing dinner that must have cost Matt a fortune. Occasionally, Maggie peeked over at Josh. She couldn't help it. When he laughed, the sound hovered above the room. He moved from table to table, talking with everybody as if he'd known them their entire lives. Jude, the paparazzi, followed Josh around, snapping pictures. When they were almost to her table, Maggie saw Josh turn and whisper something to Jude. Jude laughed, then packed away his camera.

The whole time, Brad kept up a steady stream of conversation beside her, answering questions about what it was like to travel with Joshua. "We go from town to town, mostly speaking in Worship Houses and Community Halls."

"Isn't it a rule that you have to be a member of a Worship House in order to speak there?" somebody at their table asked.

"Josh isn't about rules and religion," Brad explained. "He just wants people to have a relationship with God."

Maggie tried to listen, but her muscles twitched. She needed whatever Ben had been able to get his hands on. Besides, she'd never heard anyone talk about a relationship with God. It didn't make any sense. Why would God want a relationship with any human, especially someone like her? It was almost funny.

She stood up from the table and tossed her napkin onto her empty plate. She couldn't take this another minute. "Ben, let's get out of here."

Chapter Five

The next week passed like most weeks, days bleeding into days. Ben made a new connection, and Maggie paid him for her own supply.

At the bar, Maggie went through the motions of life, waiting until she could get back to her apartment and numb herself. Almost daily, she thought about overdosing and taking what was left of her life, but the act hardly seemed worth the effort. Besides, she'd screwed up suicide before. She'd probably find a way to screw it up again.

Andy returned her car before he closed the shop to travel with Josh. He told her that Matt was joining them, and the Sons of Thunder had left their dad's cycle business to throw in with Joshua, too.

About a week after Matt's party, Maggie was sitting with a couple of the regulars when Samantha burst through the doors of the bar. Maggie had met Sam in a recovery group, and they'd stayed in touch. Sam lived in Oberlin, about 50 miles up the road.

"Don't you answer your cell anymore?" Samantha demanded, charging at Maggie.

"Hello to you, too, girlfriend," Maggie returned.

"I called you a dozen times!"

Maggie shrugged. "Sorry. I forgot to charge the phone. Shoot me. Then tell me what's the matter."

Sam pulled up a chair close to Maggie, ignoring the men at the table. They didn't ignore her, though. Men never did. Samantha blamed her lack of girlfriends on the fact that she was biracial and didn't fit in with whites or African-Americans. But Maggie had always believed other women hated Sam because she was so extraordinarily beautiful. Her looks had probably done her more harm than good. Sam was only a year older than Maggie, and she'd already been divorced twice. She'd run through more live-ins than Maggie could count.

"Maggie, I don't know where to begin."

Maggie leaned forward, elbows on the table. She'd never seen Sam this excited. "What? What happened?"

Sam took a deep breath. "I met a man."

The guys at the table burst into laughter, and even

Maggie had trouble keeping a straight face. "A man," she repeated. "Does Ray know?" Sam's current boyfriend had a mean temper.

"Ray?" Sam looked baffled, as if she didn't see why Ray would care about this new man in her life. "I don't know. It doesn't matter. Ray's moving out."

"I see. And this new man is true love, right?" Maggie couldn't help herself. The two of them had had this conversation half a dozen times before. Sam was the only woman Maggie knew who had worse luck with men than she did.

"No!" Sam protested. "It's not like that!"

Gary interrupted. "Do you girls want us to leave you alone so you can have your girl talk?"

The other men chuckled.

"No!" Sam turned to them one by one. "I want everybody to know!"

"To know what, Sam?" Maggie asked. "Slow down. Start from the beginning."

Sam smoothed her long, wavy hair. "Okay. You know I took that job with Waterby's, right? I couldn't get anything else. Anyway, I deliver those big bottles of water to businesses all over Oberlin. It's not so bad. I put the jugs on a cart and wheel them in. The hard part is getting hit on by sleazy businessmen."

Maggie knew all this. "Cut to the chase, Sam."

"Okay. So I was delivering to the courthouse early this morning. And there was this man standing and watching me. I thought if I flirted with him a little, I might get him to help me lift the bottles onto the cart. That's the only hard part."

"Yeah?"

"He was onto me right away. He asked me for a drink, and I said something like, 'Why should I give *you* a drink?' And he said, 'If you knew who I was, you'd ask *me* for a drink and I'd give you living water—and you could drink it forever and never be thirsty again.'"

Maggie laughed. "So your new love is an infomercial salesman? What's that 'living water' go for? Only 19.95, plus postage and handling? I hope you didn't fall for it, Sam."

"Let me finish!" Sam pleaded. "I told him I'd love some of that water, especially if it meant I'd never have to haul those water bottles around anymore. And that's when everything changed."

The bar grew still, except for the buzzing from the cooler in back. Maggie could see now that Sam wasn't kidding around. Something had happened to her.

"Out of the blue," Sam continued, "he asked me to go get my husband. I gave him my best smile and told him I wasn't married. His gaze locked onto me. I don't know how else to say it. And he said, 'I know you're not, Sam. You've had two husbands, and Ray, the man you're living with now, isn't your husband.' Then he proceeded to tell me my entire life's story—everything there is to know about me, things even you don't know, Maggie! He *knew* me. I'd heard about psychics and mediums, or whatever you call them. So I asked him if he was a psychic." Sam was quiet for a minute before going on. "He said he was the Son of God!"

"Joshua," Maggie muttered, remembering what Andy had said about him.

"Yes!" Sam shouted. "His name is Joshua! How did you know that, Maggie?"

Maggie shook her head. "Go on. What happened after that?"

"Then your friends Andy and Pete and some other guys came up. So I ran all the way back to Main Street, telling everybody I passed that they should go check out the man who told me everything I ever did. I shouted it at the Dairy Queen, in the grocery store, at the library— everywhere. Then I called everybody I could think of— including you. And when you didn't answer, I ran over here. Do you think . . . do you think he could really be the Son of God?"

"Let's go see him," Gary suggested, putting his baseball cap back on. He stood up. "Come on! I'll drive."

The others guys were up for it, and Samantha told them where she'd left Joshua. As they left, she turned to Maggie. "Come with us."

"I can't." Maggie could have closed the bar for an hour easily enough, and the boss wouldn't even have known. But she didn't want to go with Sam. She didn't want to see Joshua. The last thing she wanted was to meet someone who could tell her all about her miserable, wasted life.

"Please, Maggie?" A horn honked, and Sam backed toward the door.

"You go on."

Sam stood in the doorway now. "In a minute!" she shouted to the guys. Then she turned back to Maggie. "Okay. But you have to go with me to hear him talk tonight."

"Tonight?" Maggie was already trying to think up a good excuse.

"It'll be fun! Josh is speaking in the Mud Hens' stadium after the game. Pete's pitching. Andy said he'd get us tickets and drive us there. You said you wanted to see Pete pitch."

Maggie would have liked to see a Mud Hens game. But hearing Joshua was another matter. "I don't know, Sam."

The horn honked again. This time it didn't let up.

"We'll pick you up at five. If you don't want to stay after the game, we'll find a way back. I have to go!" She ran to Gary's car and got in the backseat.

❖

After her shift ended, Maggie drove to her apartment and changed into jeans and a T-shirt. She was already starting to regret giving in to Samantha. Maggie wanted to see the ball game. It would give her something interesting to write to Chance about. But she'd hold Sam to her promise to find a ride back after the game.

Andy and Sam arrived a few minutes early in Andy's white beater pickup, and Maggie scooched into the cab with them. It was a good-sized truck, with two seats that folded down from the sides to make a tiny backseat.

"Tell Maggie who's meeting us at the game," Sam said to Andy, after making Maggie fasten her seat belt.

Andy circled the apartment parking lot and headed toward Highway 224, west toward Toledo. "Okay. Let's see. Pete got us a block of seats, so just about everybody will be there."

Maggie was feeling less and less sure about this whole

thing. She had no idea who Andy meant by "everybody." She'd smoked a joint after work and had taken two Vicodin right before she left her apartment, so she was feeling pretty decent. But she hadn't brought anything with her because she was afraid they might search purses at the ball game. Now she wished she'd risked it. Or, better yet, that she'd stayed back at her apartment with her stash, instead of heading out to meet "everybody."

Andy was listing names. Most of them Maggie didn't recognize. " . . . Thad, Phil. I guess Brad and Bob are riding their cycles. Matt's picking up Jude."

"Jude?" Maggie didn't know many Judes. "Jude Smith? The paparazzi?"

Andy laughed. "I'm not sure that's what he'd call himself. But yeah. He's been hanging around more and more. I think he's coming along on the next trip with Josh."

"I haven't met Jude yet," Sam commented. "Nate likes him, though."

"I forgot about Nate," Andy continued. "He'll be there tonight."

Maggie didn't know who Nate was, and she wasn't about to ask. For one thing, she didn't care. After tonight, she'd probably never see most of these people again, unless they came by the bar, which she didn't think was very likely. For another thing, her head was sliding into float mode from the Vicodin. Her brain had become as light as a balloon, and names and thoughts swirled together, breezing through but not sticking. That was fine with her.

Sam kept talking about the people waiting for them

at the ballpark. "Nate's a top-notch lawyer. Andy, tell Maggie what Josh said the first time you guys saw Nate."

Andy grinned at Sam, and Maggie experienced a twang of jealousy. She and Andy had never been anything but friends, so it wasn't a guy-girl jealousy thing. It was more that, even though Sam hadn't known Andy long, they already had something—some level of friendship—that Maggie didn't have with either of them.

"Josh said," Andy began, signaling before turning onto 250, "'Well I'll be. An honest lawyer!'"

Sam laughed and launched into her stockpile of lawyer jokes. Husband Number Two had been a lawyer, and not the honest kind.

Maggie tried to laugh in the right places, but the pills were peaking. Sam and Andy drifted farther away, into another world. One she was content to watch from behind a fuzzy screen.

Maggie must have dozed off because, when she opened her eyes, they were on the outskirts of Toledo. Her head was already clearing. Andy stopped the truck in front of a sky-rise office building—the kind with windows that look like mirrors, so nobody can see what goes on inside.

A short, stocky, square-shouldered man in his mid- to late thirties walked out. He wasn't dressed for a ball game and he carried a laptop, so Maggie was surprised when he kept coming toward the pickup and then opened the passenger door. He looked surprised to see Sam and Maggie already there, taking up the front seat.

Andy leaned over from the driver's side. "Sorry, Tom. Do you mind squeezing in back? We're just five minutes

Dandi Daley Mackall

from the park. Maggie, Sam, this is Tom Anderson. He's a computer analyst, and this is his first ball game."

Tom, clutching his laptop, climbed awkwardly into the back.

Sam helped him flip down the side seat. "Why don't you let me sit there, Tom? You can ride up here."

Maggie figured Sam's legs were longer than Tom's, and she'd be a worse fit in the back. Maggie would have been a better fit, but she didn't have the energy or the desire to offer to move.

Tom adjusted his laptop on his lap. "No. I'm just fine. Thank you, though."

Sam asked Tom a million questions as Andy drove them through downtown Toledo. He turned onto Erie Street, then Washington, then drove until he found free parking on Superior.

The ballpark lights stretched over the tops of trees. Maggie smelled popcorn when she climbed out of the truck and fell in beside Sam. They walked under the sign Fifth Third Field.

"Pete's pretty nervous tonight," Andy confided as they made their way to the front gate. "He can use our prayers. Tiger scouts have been searching for a new pitcher, and Pete knows the scouts will be here in full force."

"Hope he has a good game," Sam said, kind of like she doubted it.

Andy led the way toward the ticket gate and got them into the shortest line. "Pete said to meet him and Josh back by the dugout."

Maggie knew Josh would be speaking after the game.

But this was the first she'd heard about him being there for the game . . . with them. The man made her nervous. And that troubled her.

Men never made Maggie Dale nervous. It was the other way around.

Chapter Six

Maggie took advantage of their waiting time in the ticket line and whispered to Sam, "Don't forget. You promised you'd find us a way home if I don't feel like staying for the rally or whatever you call it."

"I know. But give him a chance, girlfriend, will you?" Sam waved to a couple of guys in another line. Maggie had never seen them before. They waved back.

Security officials were searching bags and backpacks. But when Andy got to the front of the line, they recognized him.

"Andy!" The white-haired ticket guard shook Andy's hand. "Hope your brother is ready for tonight. Scouts are all over the place. They're watching warm-ups."

"Pete's ready for 'em!" Andy assured him.

The guard nodded and let Maggie and Sam pass through with Andy. No search.

Mentally, Maggie kicked herself for leaving Vicodin and Percodan back at the apartment. The buzz was already gone, and she was starting to feel restless. A slight pressure had begun on the top of her head. She didn't even have aspirin on her.

"Not you, sir." The guard stopped Tom from going into the stadium with them. "What's in there?"

"A computer." Tom hugged his laptop closer to his chest, as if ready to fight for it.

Andy went back for him. "Tom's with me."

"Sorry. I'll still need to search him. We can't be too careful these days. You hear about that threat down in Columbus? Terrorist Threat level's up to orange."

"It's okay, Andy," Tom assured him.

The guard motioned Tom toward a curtained area with a folding table in front of it. Two police officers took the laptop from him.

Andy shouted over at him. "Meet us at the dugout!"

Tom waved back.

Andy led Maggie and Sam onto the field and down the line to the Mud Hens' dugout. Pete and Josh were standing in front of the dugout, but they didn't seem to notice Andy as he walked up.

Maggie was close enough to hear part of what Josh

was saying: ". . . your arm straight and don't signal the pitch. That's what you've been doing the last few games. Make the release here." Josh took the ball from Pete and demonstrated where to hold and release.

"And that's all?" Pete asked, copying the wrist motion.

Josh grinned. "That, and what I showed you about smoothing out your swing. Then just play ball and enjoy the beautiful evening." He tossed the ball to Pete. "Toss up your worries, man. There's a reason they say '*Play* ball!'"

Sam elbowed Maggie. "Exactly! That's what I've got to do. Toss up my worries. I swear, Maggie. Every time that man speaks, he changes my life."

Maggie didn't say anything. She was taking in the crisp night, the sweet smell of fresh grass, a hint of popcorn and hot dogs mingling with onions. The sky was clear, and the ballpark lights illuminated sharp figures on the field. She hadn't even noticed how calm it all was until Josh mentioned that it was a beautiful evening. He was right about that, at least.

Pete finally turned to them. "Hey, you made it! Thanks for coming, guys! Maggie, Sam, great to see you. I better get to the bull pen." He started to go and almost ran into Tom, who had finally passed security. "Tom? You brought your laptop?"

Tom shrugged apologetically, while his face reddened.

Pete laughed. "See you guys later!"

When Pete was gone, Andy turned to Josh. "Josh, have you met—?"

Joshua interrupted him and shook Maggie's hand. "Maggie and I were at the same dinner at Matt's. But we didn't exactly meet, did we, Maggie?"

Maggie was surprised that he'd noticed her there and that he knew her name. It made her suspicious. Men only paid attention when they wanted something. His warm smile should have put her at ease, but it didn't. She found that she couldn't quite look at him, not directly.

Sam stepped in and shook his hand too. She and Josh talked for a minute before Josh walked back to the dugout and Maggie and Sam took their seats. They were great seats, right above the dugout. Maggie maneuvered so she could sit between Sam and Andy. Little by little, the others arrived. Matt showed up in a Mud Hens T-shirt and a baseball cap worn backwards. Brad and Bob sat in front of Maggie and Sam, and started in on a story about something funny that had happened on their ride into Toledo when they'd raced along a stretch of deserted highway.

The pills were wearing off fast, and Maggie was having trouble focusing. Her mind kept wandering down different paths that all ended in thoughts of Chance. He should have been here, sitting next to her.

Behind her, a little boy was crying because his dad wouldn't get him a hot dog. Maggie turned around to see the boy, who couldn't have been older than four or five. For Maggie, his cry cut through every other noise in the stadium. She couldn't stand it. She wanted to buy him the hot dog herself. If Chance were here, she would have bought him anything he wanted—hot dogs, peanuts, popcorn.

Just when she thought she couldn't take another second of the boy's crying, he stopped. He jumped to his feet and cheered as the Mud Hens ran onto the field. The fans applauded each player as his name was announced over the

Dandi Daley Mackall

loudspeaker. But when the announcer called Pete's name, the fans went wild. The boy behind Maggie screamed Pete's name over and over.

Pete took the mound and threw a few practice pitches. Then the Ottawa Lynx's lead-off batter stepped up to the plate.

"This guy's good," Andy admitted. "He's hit off Pete in the last three games."

On the first pitch, the batter swung and missed. The crowd exploded into applause.

"That looked really fast from here," Sam commented. "It was a good pitch, right?"

"It was a great pitch!" Andy shouted over to her.

The batter missed the second pitch, and the third pitch was a called strike. The crowd went crazy. But it was nothing compared to what happened when the next two batters both struck out, and the top of the first ended without a hit. Mud Hens fans were on their feet, cheering Pete.

Josh stayed down in the dugout until the second inning. Then he climbed up to an empty seat next to Tom, two rows behind Maggie. Whatever he'd told Pete must have worked because Pete kept getting batters out, one after another. After the third inning, nobody on the Lynx team had gotten a hit. A couple of the outs were easy pop-ups, but most of the batters went down on strikes.

Josh was wearing a sweatshirt and baseball cap, but people began to recognize him anyway. Maggie saw them pointing at him from different parts of the stadium. Eventually, people were standing in the aisles, waiting to see him.

Around the fourth inning, weird things began to

happen. Maggie watched a middle-aged woman limp up the steps to Josh's row. She could have sworn the woman was nearly a hunchback. But a few minutes later, the same woman trotted down the steps, laughing, her back as straight as Tom the Computer Geek's.

Maggie leaned into Andy. "What just happened to that woman?"

Andy glanced over at the woman, who was sliding into her seat across the aisle. "I'm not sure exactly. It's different every time."

"You've seen this before?"

Andy nodded. "Josh has been healing people all over the state, Maggie. People with cancer. People with AIDS."

Maggie couldn't believe those stories hadn't made the news. "Why isn't Josh more famous, then? I'd think everybody would want to be healed by him."

Together they watched the woman hug the girl next to her.

"Josh probably asked that woman not to tell anybody what happened," Andy explained. "That's what he usually does."

"But why? I don't get it. Why wouldn't he want to heal the whole world if he could?"

Not that she believed any of this. The world was full of fake healers and gullible people ready to buy into anything. It was filled with men who were clever liars and women who were willing to buy into their lies.

Andy smiled at her, and something about that smile reminded her of Josh, even though the two men didn't look a thing alike. "Josh does want to heal everybody, Maggie—

physically *and* spiritually. He doesn't just care about Ohio. Joshua has come for the whole world."

"Then why wouldn't he do something internationally? Like set up clinics at the UN or get on international links or something?"

Andy grinned. "You're starting to sound like Jude. Josh says that while he's here on earth, he's only one person. His strategy is to train people like us, so we can train other people, who will reach other people. Get it? That way, the whole world will get the *whole* message, not just the healing part. If Josh becomes famous too fast, he can't do that."

Brad, in the row in front of them, must have been eavesdropping. He craned his neck around to face them. "I think Josh should run for governor."

"Yes!" Andy's eyes got big. "Pete and I have talked about it a lot. We think Josh would make a great president."

Was that what this was all about? Maggie wondered. Maybe it was some new kind of political campaign.

The crowd around Joshua grew bigger and bigger. Maggie overheard bits and pieces of conversations, with words like *cancer* and *miracle*. She wasn't sure what inning it was when Sam left and came back with hot dogs.

"So what's the score now?" Sam asked.

Josh called down to Sam, "Don't ask me. I never keep score."

Sam laughed and took a big bite of her chili-drenched dog. "You know what? Pete's gotten every single batter out, right? If he keeps this up, he could end up pitching a—"

"Don't say it!" Bob shouted. He reached back and

covered Sam's mouth with his hand. "You can't say it! Don't even think it. It's bad baseball luck."

Josh laughed out loud. "Such a big faith you have there, Bob."

"I can't believe you buy into that superstition stuff!" Brad scolded. Then the brothers argued about it until Jude told them to keep it down and watch the game.

Pete pitched a perfect game. The final score was 11 to 0, with Pete getting four hits, including a triple and a homer.

Maggie didn't know that much about baseball, but even she could tell this was something extraordinary. Bob and Brad ran down onto the field screaming louder than anybody else in the stands.

Andy's eyes teared up. "It's Josh. Josh did this for Pete."

The announcer kept saying over and over, "A perfect game! You saw it with your own eyes! Pete has pitched a perfect game!"

Maggie and Sam followed the guys onto the field.

On the mound, Pete was being lifted onto his team-mates' shoulders. He kept craning his neck, looking around until his gaze landed on Joshua. Then Pete lifted his glove and yelled, "Thank you! Thanks, Josh!"

His expression was more than grateful, more than joyful. Maggie thought she could see awe there and—but she knew this was crazy—fear.

Chapter Seven

It took quite a while to clear the field and bring in the platform where Josh would stand to deliver his message, or give his talk, or whatever he was going to do. Maggie didn't know exactly when she had decided to stay, but she wished they'd get on with it.

She thought about getting a beer. Or two. Or three. But beer never did much for her except make her sleepy. She'd have given anything for a joint and a place to smoke it.

Sam tugged Maggie with her to the side steps of the platform, where

Matt and Andy were sitting. Maggie didn't want to be so close. The last thing she needed was to be seen with Josh or connected with whatever weird things he might come up with tonight.

"Can't we go sit in the bleachers?" Maggie begged. She glanced around, surprised to see that the stadium was more packed than it had been for the game. "Sam, do you have any idea the abuse I'll get from the regulars at the bar if they see me here?"

Sam won the tug-of-war, and they both plopped onto the platform steps. "If they see you here, Maggie, that means they stayed to listen, too."

The announcer sounded like the same guy who had called the game. "Ladies and gentlemen, please find your seats as quickly as possible. Joshua Davidson will be speaking to us in five minutes!"

Right on time, Josh walked to the front of the platform. Before anyone could applaud, he waved them off and started talking. He used a microphone, but Maggie had to wonder if he really needed it. There was something about his voice that rose above the noise in the stadium, that silenced everything and everyone. She'd expected him to lecture them, like the Worship House and Community Hall leaders in services she'd gone to as a child. But he didn't.

Instead he told them stories. One was about a gardener trying to grow roses. The next was about a movie star getting the role she'd always dreamed of. Then he switched to a tale of an investment banker, then one about a factory worker and another about a checkout girl in a grocery store.

Dandi Daley Mackall

Maggie had always liked stories. At least a thousand times she'd imagined reading storybooks to Chance, with him sitting on her lap, waiting for her to turn the pages.

"Say you're on a class field trip," Josh was saying. "There you are, with a hundred kids piled into buses to visit a museum. Everybody has a great time visiting the exhibits. But when it's time to go home, you discover that one child is missing. Is that okay? Would you head for home anyway? You still have 99, right?" He laughed, and it rippled around the stadium like the wave.

"Of course you wouldn't go back without that one lost child! You'd look everywhere. You wouldn't leave that place until you found that kid. And when the lost child walked onto the bus, there would be more cheering than we heard for Pete's no-hitter tonight! That's how my Father in heaven feels when one person who's gone off on his own, one lost child, comes back."

In the second row of seats, Maggie saw a group of children who were clapping like crazy. One little boy stood out. He was clapping like the others, but his face was screwed up into a frown, as if he were straining to hear and understand in a way the others weren't.

And just like that, Maggie's mood switched tracks. She withdrew, backing away from everything—the stories, Josh's followers, Josh. Tears lined up behind her eyes and pressed on her eyeballs until she couldn't keep them in. Her body felt brittle, as if it might crack. Or break. Or shatter.

She wanted her pills. She needed them. She tried to get Sam's attention, to make Sam take her home, but Sam wouldn't turn around. All Sam's attention was directed at Josh.

"Is there anyone here who doesn't want to be happy?" Josh asked the crowd.

Nobody raised a hand.

Happy. Maggie didn't even know if she'd recognize happiness if it hit her in the face.

Josh looked down at his friends sitting around the platform. Everyone else in the stadium could hear him over the speakers, but Maggie thought he was talking to them, the ones closest around him. "Do you know what real happiness is? Happiness comes from God. God blesses you when you're poor and know that you need him. Do you know when you can feel God's comfort the best?" He paused, then answered his own question. "When you're at your lowest."

Tears streamed down Maggie's cheeks. She didn't bother to wipe them away.

"If your life is filled with tears, then laugh! I promise you that pretty soon, when you're with my Father, you won't be able to stop laughing."

Maggie didn't want to hear any more promises. Not from another man. But she couldn't turn Josh off. Of all the men she'd ever met, he was the hardest to ignore.

"I feel sorry for those of you who are rich because the only happiness you'll get in all eternity is the tiny piece you're getting now."

Maggie had never heard anything like this. What he said was backward, crazy. But nobody was laughing. He told them to be happy when they were sad, to celebrate when people hated them, to be glad they were poor.

According to Josh, Maggie thought bitterly, she should be the happiest person on earth.

"If someone slaps you," Josh continued, "turn so they can slap your other cheek. If they sue you for your house, let them have it. And toss in your car for good measure! If a person demands that you walk a mile with him, then run two."

When Josh finished, the crowd tried to rush onto the field. The security guards struggled to hold them back.

Maggie noticed a white-haired man in a Mud Hens uniform, trying to make his way through the crowd. He kept waving and shouting, but not at Josh. His gaze was fixed on Pete.

"Pete," Andy said, standing up for a better look, "isn't that Syd, your manager?"

Pete waved at the man, who kept coming.

"Pete! Pete!" cried his manager. "They called! They called you!" He stumbled past Maggie and Sam and onto the steps of the platform, until he was next to Pete and Josh. "Detroit called. You're going to play for the Tigers! They're calling your agent right now."

Pete's mouth dropped open, but nothing came out. Then he whipped off his Mud Hens cap and flung it in the air. "You're kidding me!" He grabbed Andy in a bear hug, and they danced around in circles, like little kids. "They're calling me?" Pete screamed. "I made it to the bigs!"

A flash went off. Maggie wasn't surprised to see that it was Jude photographing the moment.

Syd had trouble talking. "They . . . they want you to start right away, Pete. I always knew you'd make it."

Pete kept running his hand through his hair. "I'm going to be in the show. The majors!"

"Congratulations, Pete."

Everybody turned to Josh.

"Thanks, Josh." Pete walked over to him and shook his hand. "I couldn't have done it without you."

The die-hard fans in the stands let out bursts of cheers as word of Pete's offer traveled out like ripples from a rock tossed into a lake.

"I can't believe it!" Pete punched Brad's arm. "Can you? Can you believe this is really happening?"

Brad shook his head. "You deserve it, Pete. You've worked hard. Way to go!"

"Pete?" Josh said quietly.

Pete turned and stared at him. Josh stared back, his eyes soft. They were the only two men on the field who weren't cheering. Neither man spoke, but as Maggie looked on, it seemed like a whole conversation was taking place. The crowd faded. Maggie felt as if she were watching the only two people left on earth.

"I want you to come with me, Pete."

Pete cocked his head to one side, as if he hadn't heard right.

"Leave this, and come with me," Josh repeated.

Maggie waited for the punch line. Josh couldn't really be asking Pete to leave pro ball before he'd even had a chance at it.

Pete's face seemed to be frozen. He was a statue, unmoving and cold.

Josh's expression, on the other hand, was serene. "We'll

Dandi Daley Mackall

win lives for eternity, Pete, instead of games for an instant."
He said it softly, casually, as if he'd just asked Pete to come
get a hot dog with him, instead of asking him to give up his
lifelong dream.

Andy had stopped talking and was looking from Josh
to Pete, just like Maggie was. "Pete? Are you okay?"

Pete didn't answer. His lips were a hard line, his eyes
narrow slits. Lines had formed instantly across Pete's forehead. Maggie could read the struggle—no, the full-scale
battle—being waged inside him. She could almost feel it
herself.

Then something broke. At least that's what it looked
like to Maggie. The wrinkles on Pete's brow disappeared.
His face turned from a cold stone to a soft clay, as his jowls
relaxed and his lips parted in a grin.

He nodded. His grin grew, and he nodded again. He
turned to Andy and hugged him.

Andy looked completely baffled.

Pete turned to his manager. "Syd, tell Detroit thanks,
but no thanks."

"What?" Syd choked on the word.

"You heard me, buddy." Pete slapped the old man on
the back and kissed the top of his head.

"Pete," Syd tried, "are you sure you heard me right?
You've been called up! To the majors! You're going to play
in the big leagues, son!"

Pete grinned at the old man. "Sorry, Syd. Can't do it."

"Can't do it?" Syd raised his voice. "Can't do it?"

Pete, still grinning, shook his head. "I've got more
important things to do."

Josh tipped his cap. "Way to go, Pete!"

Andy sighed. "You're serious, aren't you." It wasn't a question. "Well, it was sweet while it lasted, huh?" He reached out and shook his brother's hand.

Bob stormed up to Pete. "Wait a minute! You can't be serious! This is too good to pass up, Pete! You can come with us later. Not now! It doesn't make any sense."

Maggie could tell Brad was trying not to argue, but he couldn't help himself. "Pete, listen. Couldn't you play for a year in the majors? Get a year's contract out of Detroit. Then you could join up with us." He looked to Josh, his gaze hopeful. "Josh, that would work, wouldn't it?"

But Pete didn't give Josh a chance to answer. "Nope. I'm coming now."

Maggie watched them as if they were aliens. Pete had waited his whole life for a break like this. And now he was turning his back on his dream, just to travel with Josh? That was crazy enough for one night. But what really threw her was the unquestionable fact that Pete looked happier than Maggie had ever seen him.

❖

Josh hitched a ride home with Andy. Maggie and Sam took the little seats in the back of the cab. After they dropped off Tom, Sam leaned into the front seat and asked Josh about some of the stories he'd told. Maggie curled up in her seat and listened to Josh's explanations. Everything had a deeper meaning. She listened until the voices became a hum, and she fell asleep.

Maggie didn't wake up until they pulled in front of her apartment building. She thanked Sam and the guys for the ride and climbed out of the truck, making sure not to look at Josh. The man confused her, more than ever after tonight, after all the promises he'd thrown around.

She walked to the back of the apartment building and started up the steps. It was weird how much she remembered of what Josh said, even though she didn't want to. He'd said he wanted people to be happy. Well, good for him. She wasn't even sure there *was* such a thing as happiness. Not in her world anyway. She thought about Pete. He sure seemed happy. So did Andy and the others. Even Samantha.

But Maggie Dale wasn't like them. And as she traipsed up the smelly stairwell to her apartment, under a cloudy sky that hid all trace of a moon, she figured that her being happy would take a bigger trick than turning water into champagne.

Maggie wanted to get by herself and take two Vicodin—just two—or maybe Oxy. Then she'd write a letter to Chance. Finally she'd have something interesting to write. She could tell him all about Pete's perfect game. She'd tell him about Pete's call to the majors and how he'd turned it down to go with Josh. She'd try to tell Chance everything she could remember about what Josh had said, too. She could write down the stories. Maybe it would help her sort out her own thoughts.

She rushed past the stinking landing to her door.

Ben was standing there. "Where've you been?" he demanded as she unlocked the door. His face was red— drunk red.

"I didn't know you were coming over, Ben." She walked past him and set her keys on the table. She'd seen Ben high before, but not like this. "I went to a Mud Hens game."

He laughed, but the tone of it made her arms stiffen and her heart speed up. "Because you're such a big baseball fan? Who'd you go with?"

Maggie willed her voice to be light and airy. "Samantha. You know her, from Oberlin?"

"That whore?" he yelled.

"Ben, Sam's my friend. Don't talk about her like—"

He came at her, and Maggie automatically stepped behind the table.

"I asked you who you were out with!"

He didn't have a right to talk to her like this. She hadn't expected it from him. For all she knew, he was married. It was none of his business what she did when he wasn't there.

"I told you," she said calmly. "I went to the game with Sam."

She saw his hands clench into fists.

"Yeah? And who else was in that pickup I saw drop you off?"

"You were spying on me?" Now she was angry. She could shout, too. "I went with friends. Andy and some others. So what?"

It was the wrong answer. The light went out of Ben's eyes. He leaped across the table and grabbed her by the neck. The force of it threw them both to the floor. Maggie's back smashed into something—hard.

"Let go of me, Ben!" she screamed. "Get out!"

"You don't tell me what to do." The words squeezed through his clenched teeth.

He slapped her. His knee was so heavy on her chest that Maggie couldn't get her breath. She tried to fight back, to scratch him, to push him off, but he was twice her size. He slapped her again and again.

Maggie stopped fighting and went to another place in her mind. In her head, she was starting that letter to Chance.

Dear Chance,
I can't wait to tell you where I've been. . . .

Chapter Eight

In the morning Maggie called in sick.
She stayed in bed all day and the next
day. Sam called several times, but
Maggie didn't answer her phone. She
was too sad and empty even to cry.
She tried writing Chance but stopped
after recounting the ball game.

When she could get herself out
of bed, she drank everything she
could find, mixing beer and wine and
whiskey. Then she smoked the last of
her pot, took the few pills she had left,
and fell into a dead sleep, hoping
she'd never wake up.

It was two days later when she forced herself to shower, dress, and drive into work. She told everybody she'd tripped on the stairs. She was pretty sure nobody believed her. But nobody cared enough to press it.

Somehow days passed into nights, and nights into days. Maggie kept her thoughts, her pain, to herself. She went through the motions of life—wiping tables, serving drinks, laughing with customers, earning those tips, then going straight back to the apartment after work and drugging herself into darkness.

❖

It was pitch-dark after her last shift at The Well when she climbed into her car . . . alone. A north wind had picked up, giving the night an unexpected chill. Maggie turned the key in the ignition.

Nothing happened.

She tried again. And again. She swore and slammed the steering wheel, banging it until her hand hurt. Then she pounded her fist on the dashboard. The glove compartment popped open. She slammed it so hard, it wouldn't stay shut. She stared at the open glove compartment, wishing she were in Ben's car.

Reaching into Ben's glove compartment.

Wrapping her fingers around Ben's gun.

Out of the corner of her eye, Maggie saw a light. It was coming from the back of the auto shop. Andy's shop had been closed since the night of the ball game. But there it was—a tiny light that hadn't been there all week.

Maggie got out of the car, kicked the door shut, and started across the street. The garage was closed, and the sign on the front door was still turned to Closed.

She pounded on the door. "Andy? Pete? Are you in there?" She banged harder, until she heard the *click* of the lock.

The door swung open. Andy stood in the doorway, grinning at her. "Maggie? I thought you were going to knock the door down."

"You're back!" It was the first piece of luck she'd had in days.

"Not for long. We're heading out again in the morning. Car problems, Maggie?"

She jerked her head in the general direction of her car. "It won't start."

Andy sighed. "I was afraid you were going to need a new starter. I've got a used one over here that should work." He crossed to the other side of the shop and reached to a top shelf. "Got it. I'll put it in for you."

"Would you?" Maggie was so grateful, she could have hugged him. "Thanks, Andy."

He grabbed a flashlight, raised the garage door, and ducked under. Maggie started to follow him to her car.

Andy called back at her, "You don't need to come, Maggie. Stay inside where it's warm."

She hadn't brought a jacket and wasn't particularly looking forward to standing around in the cold. "Thanks."

"Hey, Maggie."

The voice startled her. She turned to see Joshua. He was behind the pickup, leaning over Andy's worktable. It looked like he was sanding a strip of wood. "I like to come here sometimes. Andy lets me use his tools. I like making things with my hands."

Maggie remembered hearing that he'd worked in his father's construction business. "You were a carpenter, weren't you?"

He nodded, then glanced up at her. His eyes made her want to tell him everything—how she dreaded getting up every day, how hard it was just to get through the hours, the minutes. Everything took so much effort. And everything left her empty.

But she didn't say a word. Instead she gazed outside, where Andy had started working on her car. The flashlight he held between his teeth gave a ray of light under the hood.

"I'm the light of the world, Maggie," Josh said, still sanding the wood that looked smooth and round at the edges. "If you follow me, you won't be stumbling through the dark anymore because you'll have all the light you need."

The words surprised her. They felt as warm as light. Maggie didn't respond, but she drank in the words and waited for more.

The back door of the shop opened, and a dark figure slipped inside. Standing at the opposite end of the garage, Maggie couldn't make out who it was.

"Joshua? Joshua Davidson?" The man cleared his throat. "Are you in here?"

"Right over here!" Josh called out.

The man took several steps in. Maggie could see he was old and well dressed. She tried to back away quietly, but she bumped a shelf and knocked something off. It clanged to the ground.

The man jumped. "Who's there? I thought we were alone! Who else is here?"

"I'm sorry," Maggie said. "I'll wait outside."

"No, it's all right," Joshua murmured, not taking his gaze off the man.

With Joshua's words, the man seemed to recover.

Maggie was curious to see why anybody would be sneaking around to see Josh at midnight. So she stayed where she was.

"I'm Representative Nicholson," the man began.

Maggie recognized the name. Nicholson was the minority leader in the Ohio House of Representatives. He was also a leader in one of the largest Worship Houses in Ohio.

"Mr. Davidson," he began, "we're all well aware that God must have sent you to teach us. I think your miracles have been proof that God is with you."

Josh interrupted him. "Unless you're born again, you can never see the kingdom of God."

Representative Nicholson appeared as confused as Maggie felt. An important Worship House leader, not to mention a representative, had paid Josh a huge compliment. Why would Josh ignore it?

"What do you mean?" Nicholson asked. "I can't be born again. I'm an old man. Am I supposed to climb back into my mother's womb and be born all over again?" He gave a weak laugh.

Maggie wanted to leave. They were talking about birth, about being born. About being born again. She knew that was bogus. Nobody got a second chance to live. She didn't want to think about this.

Joshua didn't back down. "Nobody's getting into heaven without being born again. Once isn't enough. Humans give human life. But for a *spiritual* life, you need a spiritual birth."

Representative Nicholson scratched his head.

"Are you surprised that you have to be born again?" Josh exclaimed.

"Well, I've never *seen* this Spirit." The representative's voice sounded a little defensive to Maggie.

"Have you ever seen the wind?" Josh asked. "I doubt it. But you see its effects. You believe in wind. It's the same thing with people who are born of the Spirit."

Nicholson frowned. "I'm afraid I can't understand what you're saying. I'm not quite sure I even know what you mean about the wind, to tell the truth."

Josh's eyes were intense. "You're a respected Worship House leader, but you don't understand what I'm saying? If you don't believe me when I tell you about the wind and things you see every day, how can you possibly believe if I tell you what's going on in heaven?" Josh smiled at Nicholson, who stared down at the ground. "I really have come from my Father in heaven. And I'll go back again so that everyone who believes in me can go there with me."

Maggie tried to pretend she wasn't listening, but she was.

"God loved the world so much that he sent me here.

Do you know why? So that everyone who believes in me can have eternal life." He smiled at Maggie. "The light from heaven is here."

The same rush of warmth raced through her as it had when Josh had talked about being the light in the darkness.

"Some people love the dark too much. So they stay away from the light. They're afraid that the light's going to expose and judge everything they've done wrong in their lives. But there's no judgment like that waiting for those who trust me."

The words cut deep into Maggie's soul. She'd done what she did in the dark, hoping nobody else would ever know. Then she'd started living her whole life that way—in the dark, dying a little more each day, thinking nobody saw. Nobody knew. Nobody cared.

"Maggie, your car's ready." Andy walked up to her and handed her the keys.

Startled, she looked around for Representative Nicholson, but he was gone.

❅

On the drive home, Maggie kept asking herself over and over what it would feel like to come out of the darkness. To be born again.

As soon as she walked into her apartment, she sat down and wrote Chance.

Dear Chance,
Tonight I heard Josh talk about being born again. Born

again. I remember every second of having you inside me, Chance—a whole life waiting to begin, with no black marks on your scorecard. The world was going to be open to you. Anything was possible.

Could Joshua actually be offering that? A birth? A new start? Forgiveness for everything I've done in the dark, in secret? A clean newness, with the old filth washed away? Is it even possible? Could believing in Josh do that? What I wouldn't give for a real-life do-over!

Born again.

Sometimes I think I can remember being born the first time. My mother told me I cried and cried when I entered this world. I've spent the rest of my life discovering why.

But I'm afraid, Chance. You more than anyone else know what a coward I am.

Chapter Nine

The next morning Maggie woke up
early and brought in the paper to read
while she drank her coffee. She
wished she'd asked Andy about their
trip, and she thought she might find
out something about it in the local
newspaper. She leafed through the
pages, skipping the front-page story,
detailing terrorist threats and an
unexploded bomb found in downtown Columbus.

A name caught her eye: *Daniel
Tessler.* But the name was in the
obituary column. Maggie spilled her

coffee, then set her mug on the table. It couldn't be *her* Daniel Tessler. Not little Daniel. She read the paragraph:

Daniel Tessler, age seven, died of a brain tumor Monday night. He is survived by his mother, Cynthia Tessler, of 305 Samuel Street, Nankin, Ohio. Services will be held at the Worship House on Elm Street in Nankin today at 9:00 a.m.

Maggie had to read it again to take it in. Mrs. Tessler had been her eighth-grade English teacher, the only teacher Maggie had liked. If all teachers could have been like her, Maggie figured she might have done all right in school. Mrs. Tessler had trusted Maggie enough to let her babysit Daniel. He was such a cute baby, so good. Then Mrs. Tessler's husband had died in one of the planes that crashed into the World Trade Center during the terrorist attack on 9/11. Mrs. Tessler had quit her teaching job to stay home with her only child.

Maggie had to go to Daniel's funeral. She checked the clock and saw that she had under an hour to shower, dress, and drive to Nankin.

Somehow she managed to pull herself together and arrive at the Worship House just as the leader was beginning the service. She took a seat in the back of the high-ceilinged room. The high-backed chairs were velvet and cushioned and comfortable.

But there was no comfort in the words of the leader as he talked on and on about accepting this life and going on stoically. Maggie had been there, and all it had gotten her was an emptiness she'd tried to fill with whatever "this life" had to offer—alcohol, drugs, men.

She tuned out the leader and tried to replay Josh's words in her head. He'd talked about another kind of life, a spiritual life. A second birth. He'd talked about—no, he'd promised—eternal life.

When the service ended, the casket was lifted by six men. The congregation followed up the aisle and out to the steps of the Worship House. The sky had turned black and threatened rain.

Mrs. Tessler couldn't control her grief. *And why should she?* Maggie thought. There was nothing—*nothing*—sadder than losing a child. Daniel had been all the woman had in her life. Maggie stood back and watched as Mrs. Tessler's family gathered around her, crying and hugging beside the coffin.

All at once the crowd changed. Mourners grew quiet. Everyone was staring in the same direction.

Then Maggie saw him. Joshua stood at one end of the casket. Behind him were Pete and a couple of the others. Josh gazed at the coffin, then at Mrs. Tessler. His eyes glistened. Maggie didn't think she'd ever seen so much compassion.

"Don't cry." He walked beside the coffin, dragging his hand on top of the lid. The coffin bearers stood like statues, posters around a wooden bed. "Young man," Josh commanded, "get up!"

For a second, Maggie didn't know who Josh was talking to. One of the pallbearers, maybe?

Then she understood. He was talking to Daniel. Maggie held her breath.

Someone beside Daniel's mother cried, "Get that man away from here!"

Ignoring the crowd, Josh gripped the lid of the coffin and pushed it open.

Maggie didn't want to look, but she couldn't turn away. Inside the coffin, lying on a bed of white silk, was a young boy dressed in a black suit and tie, his hair smoothed back from his face. He could have been anybody. The son of anybody.

The boy opened his eyes.

Someone screamed.

Then the boy sat up.

Nobody spoke. Nobody breathed.

Maggie had to wipe her eyes with the back of her sleeve to keep watching.

Josh smiled at the boy, who smiled back at him. Maggie hadn't seen Daniel in over four years, but she would have recognized that smile anywhere. Then Josh reached into the coffin and lifted the boy out.

Slowly Josh carried Daniel to his mother. Sobbing, she took her son and kissed him, while grandparents, aunts, uncles, cousins, and friends closed in on them, touching the boy, as if making sure he was real.

"It's a miracle!" a girl hollered.

But not everybody felt that way. Maggie glanced around at the people still straggling on the steps. Some of them looked terrified.

"It's black magic!" one man shouted.

Mrs. Tessler didn't seem to care about anyone except her son. And Joshua. Over and over, she kept thanking Josh, while she hugged her only son, brought back from death.

Maggie watched Daniel and his mother, soaking up their joy. She could have watched them forever. It *was* a miracle. There was no other explanation. Josh had brought Daniel back from the dead. It was as if Daniel had been born all over again.

"*You must be born again.*"

Josh's words rushed back to Maggie. How long had it been since *she'd* felt alive? Hadn't she been dead inside, as dead as Daniel had been in the dark of his closed coffin? Josh had brought this child back to life. He'd given Daniel a second chance at life. Could he do that for her?

In her mind's eye Maggie could still see the coffin opening and Daniel sitting up, bright-eyed and smiling. Of course, Josh *could* give her this second, spiritual birth. But would he? No matter what else Joshua Davidson was— *who* else he was—he was still a flesh-and-blood man. And Maggie had promised herself that she would never trust another man. She knew that now.

But Josh was different. He wasn't just a man. He was the Son of God.

Rain fell, gently at first, then harder. The ex-mourners scattered, running to cars or back inside the Worship House.

Maggie stayed where she was. Closing her eyes, she turned her face to the heavens and let the raindrops prick her cheeks. Water showered her head and body, washing her clean. She believed what Josh had said about a new life in him, a new birth. She imagined the dirt and filth of her life rolling off her, running from her head, her shoulders, down her whole body, to her feet, and into the gutters. She laughed out loud, not caring what anybody thought of her. She couldn't wait to tell Josh.

Maggie opened her eyes and turned to him, but Josh was gone.

"Josh!" she cried, glancing furtively around for him. He wasn't there.

She took off running, not knowing if she was going in the right direction. She splashed through puddles. Her clothes were soaked. Still she kept running, loving the splash of the water on pavement, the squish of her shoes on grass.

When she came to the main street of Nankin, she ran up and down sidewalks, peering into windows. People pointed at her and laughed. She didn't care. She *had* to find Josh. She had to tell him what had happened to her, what he'd done for her.

In a restaurant on the other side of the street, she saw a group of men. One of them might be Josh. Maggie raced across the street, dodging a car. It honked at her. She slipped in a puddle, fell down, and picked herself up. She was covered in mud, and she'd skinned both knees. She dashed to the restaurant's window and peered inside.

They were there. Josh was sitting at one end of a long table. She could see Andy and Pete and some of the others with him. There was a city councilman next to Josh, and she recognized a senator and two representatives. How could she barge in on them?

But she had to. Maggie couldn't wait another minute to talk to Josh. She needed his forgiveness. She needed *him*. Her entire body dripping water from the storm, she walked inside. The carpet under her feet turned dark and splotchy.

The hostess, a young blonde with an armful of menus, stopped Maggie at the entrance to the dining room. "Excuse me, miss! You can't come in here." The girl eyed Maggie up and down, as if she were covered in garbage. "This is a private dining room. Maybe you'd like to dry off, or go home and get cleaned up first. Then perhaps—"

Maggie brushed past her and headed straight for Josh's table. He smiled up at her, almost as if he'd been expecting her. His hair and suit jacket were wet from the rain. None of the politicians at the table had a drop of rain on them. Yet they sat there, not doing anything for Joshua. The restaurant was air-conditioned. Maggie knew Josh must be cold. Freezing cold and wet.

All Maggie could think about was Josh. She wanted to make him warm. She took a napkin from the table and began to dry his face, dabbing the linen cloth on his forehead and cheeks. She ran the napkin over his hair until the cloth was too wet to do any good. Then she took the napkin from his lap and used it to dry his neck.

Maggie was hardly conscious of anyone else at the table as she knelt at Josh's feet to dry off his shoes. They were soaking wet. So were his socks. Maggie took off Josh's shoes and socks and began drying his feet, crying as she did, so grateful to be able to return even a drop of the kindness he'd shown her. When she felt him put his hand on her head, she cried even harder.

Up to now, the people at the table had kept their conversation going. Now one of the women muttered, "For heaven's sake! Does he have any idea who this woman is? *what* she is?"

Maggie looked up at the woman. She was tall, dressed in an expensive gray-striped suit, with a Community Hall–award pin on her lapel. Maggie wasn't sure if Josh had heard the woman or not. She thought about leaving. The last thing in the world she wanted was to hurt Josh or his reputation in any way. She started to get up but felt the gentle pressure of Josh's hand on her head. She settled back down. Of course she couldn't go. This was exactly where she wanted to be.

"Olivia," Josh said, addressing the tall woman, "let me ask you something."

"Go ahead," the woman answered, as if hearing from Josh was the last thing she wanted.

"A woman loaned money to two people," Josh began. "Five thousand dollars to the first man and fifty dollars to the second. It turned out that neither of the men could repay the loan, so the woman decided to forgive them both. She canceled their debts. Which one do you think loved her more after that?"

The woman answered right away. "I suppose the one with the larger canceled debt."

"Exactly!" Josh agreed. Then he turned to Maggie, while still speaking to the tall woman. "You know, from the minute we came into your dinner meeting, you could see that I was wet from the rain. But you didn't try to help. You didn't offer me a jacket. You didn't point out a place where I could have dried off."

Maggie felt his hand on her head again.

"But this woman, Maggie, since she first walked in, all she's done has been to try to make me comfortable, no matter how it made her look to you. I'm telling you that her sins—and there are a lot of them—have been forgiven. That's why she shows me this kind of love. But someone who doesn't feel she has much to be forgiven for only has a little love."

There were murmurings around the table. "Who does he think he is, going around and forgiving sins?" asked the councilwoman.

Josh leaned down, took Maggie's elbows, and lifted her to her feet. "Maggie, you've been fighting your own demons all these years. I know them. I know all about your deepest secrets. Now you can leave them behind you. Your faith has saved you. Go in peace."

Maggie was overwhelmed with gratitude that Joshua had forgiven her. It was too much to comprehend. She let herself feel it, let the claws inside her unclench and float out of her. For the first time in years and years, she didn't want a drink, a pill, a hit. She didn't need it. Those things had never come close to making her feel what she was feeling now.

Forgiven.

Loved.

Free.

She thanked Josh again and again as she backed out of the restaurant, oblivious to everyone but him. Then she walked back to her car in a gentle mist and a thunder that no longer scared her.

Chapter Ten

The next morning, sun streaked through Maggie's window. She was sure she'd never seen anything as beautiful as the sunshine and patch of blue sky she glimpsed through the fire escape outside her window.

She cleaned her house, flushing away pills, powder, and weed, pouring out whiskey, dumping beer cans.

All she wanted was to be with Josh—but not in the way she'd wanted to be with other men. This wasn't at all like that. Maggie wanted to soak up Josh's essence, to be more like him, to let him rub off on her. She wanted to learn more about him and more about the Father who sent him.

When she pulled up in front of the bar for work, she saw Andy jogging toward her from across the street. He handed her a package. "I want you to have this, Maggie." It was a copy of the Scriptures. "When you read it, it will feel like this has been written for you, even though it was written hundreds of years ago. You'll see."

She took the package and hugged it to her chest. "Thanks, Andy. I'll read it. I promise. I didn't even want a hit last night or a pill this morning. I don't need a drink either. It's a miracle, isn't it?"

He smiled at her. "That's great, Maggie. You bet it's a miracle. But I think Josh would tell you that you may want a drink someday. Or a pill."

Maggie stopped smiling. A too-familiar fear crept in. She didn't want this to be like her times in rehab. After rehab, she'd always stayed clean for a few days. Then she'd gone right back to it, worse than ever. "What are you telling me, Andy?"

"You might want those pills," Andy explained, "but you won't have to give in. You have the Spirit of God in you now, Maggie. You have the power to say no. You didn't have that before."

Maggie felt the relief of this promise. Without thinking, her mind, or her heart, said thank you to God.

"Anyway," Andy said, "I wanted to get this to you before we took off."

"You're leaving again? Already?"

He nodded. "Josh says we've got people to see. You take care, Maggie."

Maggie put the Scriptures into the backpack she always carried, the one with her letters to Chance. Then she walked back to the bar.

She was surprised to find the door unlocked. Her boss was sitting at a table with a few of the regulars. "Maggie! Come and join us, honey. Have one on the house."

Maggie knew her boss had been drinking because it was the only time he ever offered her a free drink. She shook her head and walked behind the bar counter. Dozens of bottles lined the shelves below the mirror. The stench of scotch and rum had never seemed so strong. Whiskey, and all that came with it, reeked from the bar, the tables, the chairs, the men.

Boss Wells patted his knee. "Don't be so unsociable."

The others chuckled in agreement.

She turned to face them, studying their hard, lined faces.

"What's got into you, Maggie?" her boss demanded. "You don't even look like yourself, girl."

"I *am* myself!" The answer was automatic. Something was rising inside her, like champagne bubbles. Joy? Was this what it felt like? And just like that, she knew she couldn't do this. Not anymore.

"Boss, for the first time in my life, I am myself!" Maggie grabbed her backpack and slung it over her shoulder. "I quit!"

She threw her key on the bar and raced outside, just as Andy was backing the pickup out of the garage. She saw Pete and Josh in the cab and Bob and Brad piled into the backseat.

Maggie ran after them, waving her arms. "Wait! Wait for me!"

She leaped into the back of the truck and settled in. "I'm coming with you."

Part 2

Chapter Eleven

Dear Chance,

It's been a couple of weeks since I wrote you a letter. But I've written you every day in my head. It's hard to explain what's happened to me. I've been born again, Chance. Born of the Spirit. That's how Josh put it, and that's how it feels. It's like the old Maggie died, and everything is new. You know better than anyone how much I wish I could change my past. But I can't. So I'm doing what it takes to change my present and my future. I quit my job at the bar to follow Josh. I've sold my television, radio, microwave—pretty much everything I have. And I don't miss any of it.

I promised you I'd always tell you the truth, so I have to admit that, even now, life isn't exactly perfect. I haven't had a drink or a pill since the day before Daniel Tessler's funeral. But I've come real close twice.

I'm not sure how much I contribute to the group. So far I mainly help with the meals or setting up camp. We stay with friends sometimes. When Josh speaks in Community Halls or Worship Houses, someone there usually puts us up for a night.

We're on the road a lot. A few of us ride in Andy's pickup. Others carpool. A lot of people have families and commute, driving to meet up with us in different towns all over Ohio.

I guess I get along with everybody, but I'm not quite one of them. Not like Jessica and Krystal anyway. They're nice enough, but I avoid them. In high school, I always had a boyfriend, never girlfriends. Jessica and Krystal are definite chicks. They could talk all day and night to each other. They don't have a problem with talking to strangers about Josh either, the way I do.

I'm still not the Maggie I want to be, Chance. I know Josh has forgiven me—for the men, the drugs, the lying, the cheating—and not because of anything I've done. It's all because of what he's doing. But I admit that when it comes to you, I can't forgive myself. I should probably talk to Josh about you one of these days, but

Dandi Daley Mackall

I haven't quite been able to. Maybe the old Maggie isn't as dead as I thought she was.

Loud voices made Maggie put away her letter. Jude and Josh were arguing—or rather, Jude was arguing and Josh was supplying short answers in a normal voice. It was a one-sided argument.

Andy had driven them to the Cleveland Metropark that morning to get away from the crowds. For over an hour, Maggie had been sitting in the back of the pickup, writing Chance in the shade of a big maple tree. She hadn't even noticed when Josh and Jude had walked up.

Jude now leaned against the pickup, apparently trying to keep Josh from getting in the driver's side. "You can't do this!" he shouted, inches from Josh's face. "I lined up a prime-time network interview for you. The cameras are all set up. They're counting on this! Think of the exposure, Josh!"

Next to Jude, Josh appeared completely calm. He put his hand on Jude's shoulder. "I promised a study group in Ashland that I'd come and talk to them. And there's a woman in Loudonville who really needs to see me."

Jude jerked back from him. "So you're talking about what? Twenty people? Thirty? I'm talking about thousands! Millions!"

Josh moved past him and opened the truck door. "I have to go where my Father tells me to go, Jude. That's why I came."

Maggie loved the way Josh talked about God as his Father. He encouraged them to do the same. Josh called them all brothers and sisters. In a way, she understood. These people were her family now. She wanted to pull out Chance's letter and write down this new thought, the sensation of what it could mean to have a spiritual family. But Matt had already teased her about writing to an old boyfriend. Maggie didn't want any of them to know about Chance.

A few yards away, a BMW wheeled into the parking lot. Maggie was pretty sure it belonged to Jessica Sanders, one of the benefits of being a senator's trophy wife. The car stopped short, without making it to a parking spot, and Jessica hopped out and ran toward them. Maggie could tell she'd been crying.

Jude stopped arguing. Pete, Andy, Matt, and the others walked up. It was as if they could all sense it. Something was wrong.

Jessica didn't stop running until she reached Josh. "Have you heard about John?"

"Crazy John?" Matt asked. "We know they arrested him. Now what?"

Several days earlier, the police had arrested John for loitering and being a public nuisance. But it was a trumped-up charge, and everybody knew it. John had called out Senator Harold in public for unfair influence and dirty business deals, and for his constant adulterous affairs. The media had reported the whole thing, and John had been thrown in jail the next day.

"They killed him," Jessica said.

"They what?" Matt stared at her.

Maggie heard the words, but she couldn't accept them.

Crazy John was the kind of character who lived forever. He was harmless. "Why? Why would anybody kill him?"

Pete exploded. "We can't let them get away with this!"

Brad and Bob started talking to Pete at the same time. Maggie heard words like *guns* and *force* and *Columbus*— enough to know they were plotting to get even.

All Josh did was raise his hand and motion for Jessica to continue. But his eyes were filled with tears. Everybody quieted down.

"Someone in John's holding cell stabbed him over and over again," Jessica explained, choking on the words. "One of the prison guards who's a follower of Josh said there's more to it than being on the wrong end of a prison fight."

Pete kicked at the gravel. "I knew it!"

Jessica kept going. "The warden removed the guards. Nobody will say where the prisoner got the knife. They took him off to solitary before anybody could talk to him."

Maggie bit her finger so she wouldn't scream or cry. She could picture Crazy John standing in front of the bar as she'd tried to hurry past him. John had made her look at herself and admit—at least to herself—how much she needed help. He'd gotten her ready to hear and understand Joshua. She should have stood up for him when people at the bar made fun of him. She didn't even know if he'd heard that she'd joined up with Joshua. She hoped he had.

"When people saw Crazy John," Josh said quietly, "they didn't see a well-dressed man living the life of luxury. They saw a prophet. The Scriptures talk about John. Did you know that? He was the Elijah who came before me to get the world ready. I'm telling you, there was nobody on earth finer than John."

Without a word, Josh wandered back into the park and disappeared. Nobody followed him. They knew where he was going and why. To get by himself and pray.

"Maybe he should have prayed before they killed John," Miguel muttered.

Maggie was surprised to hear him speak. He was the only person traveling with them who was quieter than she was. Miguel had been a migrant worker before he found Josh. He had six kids, but he came whenever Josh needed him, and he met them in most cities to help out.

Jessica turned toward him. "Miguel, you know better than that." Her voice was sympathetic, not angry. "I wish I understood more about Josh and the Father's work on earth. But I do know that there's evil in the world, just like there's good. Evil people do evil things, and it's not Joshua's fault."

Miguel looked close to tears. Jessica reached out and hugged him. They sobbed quietly together, holding on to one another.

Jude kicked a crinkled pop can that was lying in the dirt. "What's going on with Josh? with us? What are we really doing? I thought we'd be further along by now. I thought we'd be building a new world. Instead they just kill John and get away with it?"

"Jude's right!" Bob was pacing in the gravel, stirring white clouds of dust. His face was red and beaded with sweat. "Maybe we should—"

A cell phone went off. They all checked, but nobody

looked surprised when it was Bob's. Bob and Brad's mom, Sally, called every day to check on her boys.

Bob flipped his cell open and glanced at the number. Then he answered. "We're okay, Mom. Yeah, we heard. I know." He listened for a while. Brad came over and put his ear to the phone, too. "No," Bob said. "We haven't asked him yet."

"Tell her we will," Brad whispered.

"We'll do it," Bob said into his cell. "It's just not a good time right now, Mom." He finished the conversation and stuck his cell back into his pocket.

Everybody wandered into the park, splitting into pairs or small groups. Jessica followed Maggie to a picnic table under a big oak. Andy and Matt stopped to make sure they were both all right. Then they walked off into the woods, probably to pray together.

Maggie wanted to be alone. She sat on the picnic bench and closed her eyes.

Jessica sat down across the table from her. "John was a good man. Did you know him very well, Maggie?"

Maggie opened her eyes and shook her head. She could have told Jessica about the times Crazy John had talked to her in front of the bar, how he'd seen through her. She could have said that she wished she *had* known John better. But she hadn't wanted to then. She hadn't been willing to see herself through his eyes. She changed the subject. "Do you really think John was killed on purpose?" Saying it out loud made it sound like the plot of a bad movie. "Could something like that really happen in Ohio?"

"I wouldn't doubt it for a minute," Jessica answered.

"There are some powerful politicians in this state, Maggie. Senator Harold was behind John's arrest. It doesn't take much imagination to believe he's responsible for John's murder, too. My husband says that Senator Harold has more power in this state than the governor does. Those two men hate each other."

"They're from opposing parties, right?" Maggie didn't pay much attention to politics, but you couldn't live in Ohio without hearing about Senator Harold and the governor.

"It's deeper than just being from opposing parties," Jessica explained. "I'm not sure how it all started, but they've been feuding ever since my husband took office. I know that much. We can never have the two of them at the same party."

"If they could arrest John, could they do it to Josh?" It was the first time Maggie had been afraid for him. "Do the politicians hate him, too?"

"It depends on the day." Jessica put her elbows on the picnic table and rested her head on her hands. Then she smiled at Maggie.

Maggie relaxed a little. Jessica was married to a politician. If she wasn't worried about Josh, then Maggie didn't need to worry either. She shifted around on the bench, tucking her feet under her, and tried to return Jessica's smile. Maggie wondered if this was what it had been like for high school girls at sleepovers, when they'd stayed up all night talking about boys.

"My husband didn't like John," Jessica admitted, "but I don't think he's made up his mind about Josh yet." Her finger traced the chipped white paint on the picnic table.

"I'm going to miss John. I loved his honesty, his boldness. I wish I could be half as brave as he was."

"Me too," Maggie muttered. She glanced over her shoulder. The group was scattered around the area, sitting under trees and at other picnic tables. There was no sign of Josh, though. He might stay out all night praying. They never knew.

She turned back to Jessica. "What do you tell your husband when you come here?" As soon as she'd asked, she wished she hadn't. It wasn't any of her business. She wasn't any good at girl talk. "I'm sorry. I didn't mean to pry."

"No. It's a good question." Jessica smiled at her again. "I tell him some things, but probably not enough. He doesn't approve of my being away from Washington so much. But it's more than that. The senate's starting to take sides over Joshua, and my husband wouldn't want to get caught on the wrong side. They've had some pretty big fights over Josh."

Maggie thought of the roundtable discussion she'd heard on TV. One party had claimed Josh's support on one issue, and the other party claimed he endorsed *their* issue. "So what does your husband do when they're arguing about Josh?"

"He tries to stay in the middle of everything, I'm afraid. He doesn't want to get involved in religion if he can help it. And he tries very hard to keep me from getting into it too."

Maggie stared at the woman across from her, as if she'd never seen her before. Maggie had always envied Jessica's life. Everything seemed to come so easily to her.

She'd been voted "Most Likely to Succeed" in high school, graduated from college in three years, and gone on to marry a rich senator. She'd gotten out of Slayton, Ohio. But it couldn't be easy supporting a man your husband disapproved of. Jessica could have stayed in DC and had everything most women dream of. Instead she managed to spend almost as much time with the group as Maggie did.

"I think you're pretty brave to be here at all," Maggie murmured.

"Me? I'm not brave!" Jessica protested.

"I don't know if I'd be brave enough or unselfish enough to leave the kind of life you must have in Washington," Maggie admitted. "I didn't exactly have much to keep me in Slayton."

Jessica was quiet for a second. Then she asked, "How's your mother, Maggie?"

Maggie had no idea how to answer. What was she supposed to say? That her mother refused to talk to her? That her mother was probably celebrating the fact that her daughter was out of sight now, as well as out of mind? "I don't know." She changed the subject fast. "What else do they say about Josh in Washington?"

Jessica nodded, and Maggie got the feeling she understood that Maggie didn't want to talk about her mother. Jessica rolled her shoulders, as if her neck was stiff. "Let's see . . . one senator will hear that Josh said something about the earth belonging to the poor, so he's all for Joshua Davidson and a tax hike on the rich. Then word will filter down that Joshua is against abortions, and that same senator suddenly decides that Josh is a crazy man who needs to be put away."

Maggie was jerked out of her connection with Jessica at the mention of abortion. She could almost feel the wall between them growing back. She and Jessica could never be girlfriends, and Maggie was foolish to think they could. What good, pure Jessica knew about the ugliness and pain of abortion was nothing compared to Maggie's firsthand knowledge, a knowledge that was with her every day. She wanted to get away from Jessica, to run into the woods where she could write Chance and tell him one more time how sorry she was.

Maggie pushed herself from the picnic table. The bench tipped over as she got out, and she swore, struggling to get her foot free.

"Maggie, are you all right?" Jessica asked.

"I'm fine! I just . . . I just need to . . ." She grabbed her pack. She had to get away. Maggie took off running. She ran until she couldn't breathe. Panting, she dropped to the grass and rifled through her pack for a piece of paper and a pen. She ripped the paper as she yanked it out and swore again, fighting back tears.

Dear Chance,
I know I've told you how sorry . . .

But she couldn't stop her hand from shaking. She couldn't write. She couldn't see the page. So she shut her eyes, but it didn't help. She couldn't stop her mind.

Chapter Twelve

Maggie leaned against the trunk of the
nearest tree. Images flashed behind
her eyelids, and she couldn't stop
them from playing. She saw herself,
two months pregnant, sitting in Alan's
car at the reservoir outside of Slayton,
the very place they'd conceived the
baby Alan knew nothing about.
Nobody knew, even though Maggie
had been throwing up before school
in the mornings. It wouldn't be long
before her mother caught her and
figured out why.

Alan had driven her to the reservoir after their senior prom. . . .

Maggie knew how he'd pictured the rest of the night. He'd come prepared with blankets and pillows this time.

"Come on, Maggie," he pleaded, coming around to her door and trying to coax her into the backseat. He'd already had two beers from the cooler. "I'm going off to school in a couple of months. We have to make every minute count, babe."

He hadn't even pressed her for a reason when she'd told him that her own plans for college had changed, and she wouldn't be joining him at Kent State in the fall. She'd almost told him right then that she was pregnant. But she hadn't. She'd known him well enough not to tell him.

"Maggie, have a beer." He ran to the trunk and got each of them a can. He popped the top off a lukewarm can and held it out to her. "You gotta loosen up, babe. Take it!"

This had been one of the reasons they hadn't been getting along. Maggie was trying to stop drinking and smoking. She'd learned in health class what that did to unborn babies. She hadn't wanted to hurt Chance. In her mind, she'd already named him. She'd known it was a boy from the first moment the pregnancy test, which she'd used in a gas-station toilet, came up positive.

Maggie shook her head, refusing to take the can Alan shoved in her face.

He swore at her. "Why are you acting like this? You're no fun anymore. Why can't you just take the beer?"

"Because I'm pregnant, Alan."

He stepped away from her, as if she'd said she had AIDS. "Quit screwing around, Maggie." He tried to laugh it off. He opened his own beer and took a long swig.

"I'm pregnant. Did you hear me? I'm—"

"You can't be pregnant!"

"I can, and I am."

He ran his fingers through his thick brown hair. She loved his hair. She loved running *her* fingers through it. His breathing got deeper. His chest heaved. Maggie was afraid he might have a heart attack, a stroke, or something. She started to get out of the car, to go to him.

"You don't know it's mine." He spat out the words, lifting his chin, as if daring her to prove it.

Maggie wanted to die. When she could speak, it was in a whisper. "How can you say that to me?"

"Do you?" he shouted. "You can't prove it's mine!"

"I'm two months pregnant," she said, feeling like a slut who needed to pinpoint which man she'd slept with when. Alan hadn't been her first. She was sure he'd known that. High school boys never kept their sexual conquests secret unless they didn't have any. But she hadn't even looked at another guy since she and Alan had been together. "This baby is yours!" she screamed.

"Don't call it a baby!" He paced away from the car.

Maggie was scared that he wasn't coming back. That he'd leave her there. By herself. Without anybody.

But 10 minutes later Alan came back. And somewhere, somehow, while he'd paced the grassy hills of the reservoir, he had made up his mind. He climbed into the driver's seat and calmly declared, "Get rid of it, Maggie. It's no big deal.

My cousin's girlfriend did it. It was over in, like, fifteen minutes or something."

Maggie stared at him, her heart freezing slowly. It wasn't that this was a new idea to her. An abortion had been the first thing she'd thought of as she'd left that gas station, knowing her whole life had changed. Even before then, while she'd read the directions on the home-pregnancy box, while she'd gathered the "evidence," while she'd carried the kit out to the Dumpster so Ray, the gas guy, wouldn't see it, she'd told herself that this "mistake" didn't have to ruin her life. This was the twenty-first century, after all.

But a week went by. And then another. And another.

Maggie had checked out library books on pregnancy and babies, hiding the books in her pack, leaving them in her school locker. She'd been amazed, looking at the pictures of fetuses just a few weeks old. They didn't look like a bunch of cells. They looked like tiny babies. She'd learned that Chance's heart was already beating.

She'd started thinking of him as Chance, even though she didn't know anybody by that name. It seemed to her as if Chance had just named himself.

And so she'd put off making a decision. She'd put off telling Alan . . . until that night.

Alan started the car and kept talking. "It's your life and all. You know—your body and whatever. So it's up to you. But you ought to do it as soon as possible, right? You haven't told anybody, have you?"

"I told you," Maggie answered softly.

"'Cause some people get all weirded out about this stuff." He backed up the car, then pulled onto the dirt lane.

They drove slowly, passing couples in other dark cars. Maggie stared at the moon, a half-moon, and wondered if anybody had ever felt as alone as she did. . . .

Alan had dropped her off, then dropped her from the face of his world. At school he barely spoke to her. He rushed out after classes instead of giving her a ride home. When a week went by and she hadn't heard from him, she called him. And called him.

He didn't call back.

The same day that Maggie learned Alan was dating Alexa, Maggie's mother found out Maggie was pregnant. When the school nurse had found Maggie vomiting in the bathroom, she'd sent her home. Maggie had walked into her house, and her mother had slapped her across the face and asked only one question: "How could you do this to me?"

The next day her mother drove her to the Family Planning Clinic. Maggie had actually chuckled at the name, which only worked if every family entering its doors planned to end the life of its newest family member.

Maggie had tried every day since to blot out the memory of that day. But the images had grown sharper, if anything. . . .

The antiseptic smell of the waiting room.

Her embarrassment undressing in the tiny, cheery room that made the abortion feel like acting, as if the whole thing were happening to someone else and she was just dressing up to play the part.

Her mind still carried a snapshot of the silver tools of the trade, set out on a cart, like milk for school lunches. She couldn't remember the pain, but she couldn't forget the empty horror when it was over. She'd never gone back to school.

Now, sitting in the grass of the Cleveland Metropark, her pen still clutched in shaky fingers, Maggie thought she could still feel Chance inside her. She didn't, of course. Couldn't. Maybe she never had. She'd read in the books that mothers couldn't feel their children move as early as she'd thought she did. But she'd also read that they did move. In the sixth or seventh week, they moved. And that's what she'd imagined she'd sensed . . . was sensing now.

But maybe she did feel him, or the memory of him. One of the few things she remembered from science class was the discussion about light-years. From earth, the things we see happening in the far-off sky really happened years and years ago—light-years ago. But to us, they're happening now. Chance was like that—gone, over, yet happening again and again to her.

On the other hand, Maggie thought, maybe what she was feeling wasn't Chance. It was his absence.

Chapter Thirteen

A horn honked three, four, five, six
times. Maggie dried her eyes and
zipped up her pack. Behind her, the
horn blared again. She took a minute
to get herself together, grateful that
Jessica hadn't tried to follow her.
Maggie needed the time alone.

She glanced up the hill and
spotted Josh walking down, heading
toward the parking lot. At least a
dozen people surrounded him. From
the looks of the crowd jostling him

from all sides, Josh hadn't gotten the time alone *he* needed to grieve for Crazy John.

Matt, Andy, and the others came from all parts of the park to see what the commotion was. They converged in the gravel parking lot, where a giant RV sat in the middle of the place, honking and honking. Maggie tried to see inside, but the windows were dark. Then out of the driver's seat stepped Krystal.

Jessica ran up to Maggie and took her arm, as if nothing had happened between them. "Come on, Maggie! Let's go see!" She dragged Maggie with her down to the parking lot.

Pete was inspecting the monster vehicle. "You've got to be kidding me!"

The other guys circled the RV, scoping underneath, opening the door, checking out the inside. They made sounds like little boys.

"It's for you guys!" Krystal declared, on the verge of a full-fledged cheer. "For all of us! Now we can travel together when we need to. And we can take turns sleeping in here, too. It's got beds and everything!"

Maggie stood outside the RV, while Jessica and everybody took turns crowding inside. She wished she had money like that so she could give Joshua a gift like this. It was exactly what he needed, what they all needed.

Josh strolled over to Krystal and hugged her. So did Jessica. Josh said something to the women, but Maggie was too far away to hear. Then the three of them laughed.

A young man got out of a Mercedes that was parked behind the RV. Maggie hadn't even noticed the car until now. The guy wore an expensive suit and looked like he belonged anywhere but a Cleveland city park. He walked up and stood by Krystal. Maggie wondered if Krystal's husband knew about this mystery man. In high school, Krystal hadn't been known for her monogamous relationships.

"Joshua, this is William Boyd of the Boyd Corporation," Krystal said, introducing him. "Bill, this is the man I've been telling you about, Joshua Davidson."

Maggie knew the Boyd name. She was looking at one of the richest men in the country, in the world even. She couldn't believe he was so young.

"Bill has been wanting to talk with you," Krystal explained.

Josh shook the man's hand and held it a minute before letting him go.

"Mr. Davidson, sir," the man began, "I'll get right to it, if you don't mind. What I want to know is, what kind of good things do I have to do to get eternal life?"

Josh smiled warmly at him. "Why are you asking me what's good? No one is good enough except God. But if you want an answer to your question, then you'll have to keep every commandment to receive eternal life."

"Which ones?" he asked.

"All of them. Don't murder. Don't commit adultery. Don't steal. Don't lie. Honor your parents. Love your neighbor as yourself."

Boyd looked puzzled.

At first Maggie had suspected that this rich big shot was putting them all on. Maybe he just wanted to meet the famous Joshua so he'd have a good story to tell his business partners, not to mention his girlfriends.

But she was starting to change her mind about him. He sure looked sincere.

"I've kept all those commandments," he said. "What else? There has to be something else I can do!"

Josh answered slowly. "If you want to be perfect, then go and sell all you have and give the money to the poor. Then you'll be really rich in heaven. And you can come with us."

Boyd's eyes misted with tears as he stared at Josh for what seemed like minutes. Then, hanging his head, he turned and shuffled back to his car.

As they watched Boyd drive away, Maggie saw tears in Josh's eyes, too. It amazed her how quickly Josh could care deeply for virtual strangers. It was as if he'd already loved them, even before he met them.

"No one can keep all the commandments," Josh explained. "Breaking them happens in the heart. If you hate someone, you're guilty of murder. If you lust for someone, then it's the start of adultery. The love of money makes men greedy. The truth is that it's hard for a rich person to get into heaven. Do you know how hard?" He turned to Krystal. "It's as hard as driving your RV through a buttonhole."

"You've got to be kidding!" Pete blurted out.

"No way!" Tom exclaimed. He stood next to Pete, a head shorter at least, his laptop case slung over his shoulder.

Brad was the last to turn his gaze from the dust of the vanishing Mercedes. "If that's true, then who in the world can get to heaven?"

"Nobody," Josh said. "It's impossible." His eyes twinkled, though, like they did when he told them a story he knew they wouldn't get at first but would beg him to explain later. "But with God, everything's possible!"

Maggie wasn't sure she understood, but she believed him. She knew she wasn't going to heaven because of anything good she'd done. She would just have to trust Josh to get her there, to do the impossible.

Pete spoke up again. "Some of us have given up everything to follow you, Josh. What will we get out of it?"

Josh clapped him on the back. "I promise that when I sit on the throne in the New World, you will be right there with me! And everyone who's given up houses or brothers or sisters or father or mother or children or property or anything for my sake will get a hundred times as much back, not to mention eternal life."

Maggie glanced around her at the odd mix of people standing there in the parking lot of the Cleveland Metropark. Most of them *had* given up a lot. The Sons of Thunder had left their dad's motorcycle shop to follow Josh. Pete had given up his dream of baseball, while his brother, Andy, closed down his auto shop. And they weren't the only ones who'd sacrificed. Matt hadn't just given up his lucrative drug trade. He'd emptied his offshore accounts, sold his house, his cars—everything—and given the money to build a youth center in Cleveland.

Maggie looked from Nate, the lawyer; to Phil, the high school teacher; to Tom, the computer geek. They'd all given up great jobs for Josh. Thad, another of the regulars, had stepped down as CEO of the biggest insurance company in Ohio and given up a half-million-a-year salary. Jessica and Krystal were taking time away from their husbands to be with Josh. Even Jude, the paparazzi; Miguel, the migrant worker; and Mick, the ex-leader of a tiny Worship House, had given up friends and time with family to throw in with Josh.

Only Maggie had jumped aboard without any sacrifice. She hadn't left anything or anybody behind.

Jessica and most of the guys raced to the RV.

"I'll drive!" Matt volunteered.

"Only if you promise to keep the speed limit," Krystal teased.

Maggie walked back to Andy's truck by herself. The day was warm, and she wanted to ride in the back of the pickup. They did that sometimes. She loved the sound of the wind. And she never had to make small talk, like she would have to in the RV.

She started to climb in the back of the truck when Josh stopped her. "Maggie, you can ride in the cab with us."

If it had been anybody else, she wouldn't have done it. But she climbed inside and took the backseat with Tom. Immediately he opened his laptop and started hitting keys. They'd discovered that this area of the park was a wireless hot spot, and Tom had taken advantage of that fact and spent hours on the Internet, while the rest of them slept.

Pete slid into the driver's seat and glanced back at Tom. "You're checking e-mail again, aren't you, Tom?" He winked at Josh. "Josh, I think Tom's addicted to e-mail. You better have a talk with him."

"Hey! I'm just checking headlines and weather, thank you very much." Tom replied.

Maggie enjoyed, maybe even envied, the way Pete and

Tom could joke back and forth. They hadn't known each other until they met Josh, and the two were nothing alike. But they acted like brothers.

Josh turned to the backseat. "Tom, put my name into a search engine and see who people say I am."

"You got it!" It didn't take Tom long to get results.

Maggie leaned over and checked the screen. "Wow! You got 23,900,007 hits!"

Josh didn't seem impressed. He waited for the information he'd asked for.

"Okay," Tom began. "This guy's written an article saying that you're really Elijah, the prophet." He scrolled down and tried a few of the sites listed. "Some of these people think you're Jeremiah. Some vote for Hosea. Here's one for Micah."

Tom grew quiet, while he scrolled through one long bulletin-board site. When he spoke again, his voice was solemn. "This guy thinks you're Crazy John come back to life."

They were all quiet for a minute.

Then Tom continued, "You should see all of these Worship House and Community Hall Web sites, too. A whole bunch of them think you're the devil, Satan himself."

It turned Maggie's stomach. She was convinced that there were people in the world who would believe anything, and people who believed nothing. "Turn it off, Tom," she begged, sick of the lies people wrote about Josh.

Tom logged off and closed the lid of his computer.

"Well, who do you say I am?" Josh asked.

Before any of them could answer, Pete blurted out, "You're the Son of the living God."

"You're right, Pete!" Josh exclaimed. "My Father in

heaven revealed that to you. You didn't get it from any human or from the Internet or from anywhere else." He punched Pete in the arm. "Way to go! Solid, Pete! I can build my church on this solid ground. And I'm telling you that even the powers of hell won't be able to stand up against it!"

Funny, Maggie thought. Josh actually seemed to be *building* Pete. Josh spent more time with him, and with Brad and Bob, than with the rest. Pete and Josh had long talks, and Josh saw to it that Pete and the Sons of Thunder were with him when he healed people. Maggie had to admit that she'd wondered more than once about it. If it had been up to her, she would have picked Andy instead of Pete. She liked Pete, but he was impulsive and could jump into things without thinking. She wondered if Josh could see past who Pete was and envision who he *could* be.

They drove for a while. Then Josh started telling stories about Crazy John when he was a teenager. Pete was heading north on I-71, when he interrupted. "Um . . . where exactly are we headed?"

Josh leaned back in the seat. "We're going where people are hungry."

Chapter Fourteen

Maggie gazed out the window as they got closer to the city. Wildflowers covered the roadsides, turning into patches of purple, then bright red. The air-conditioning was on, but she asked Andy to roll down the window and let in fresh air and the warmth of the sun. She heard birds singing in trees . . . so many trees. Geese honked wildly overhead, as if they were all trying to hit the same high note but couldn't reach it.

Tom shouted over the rush of the wind from the open window, "I think

we should plan to get something to eat before we go anywhere else today. And, Josh, you could use a new suit for that
Columbus meeting. Jude said we're running low on funds
again, although I don't know where it's gone. How are we
going to pull enough together to—?"

Josh laughed. It was so unexpected that Tom stopped
in midsentence. "Don't worry about little things," Josh
began, "like if we'll have enough to eat or get the right
clothes." He pointed out the window, where Maggie had
been watching the world pass by. "Look! Do you see that
cardinal there? or that sparrow? Or over there! A plover.
Those birds don't have money, do they? Do they look worried? No! Because your heavenly Father feeds them. Think
about it. Aren't you worth more to your Father than the
birds are?"

Turning around to face Tom, Josh asked, "Besides, how
much good can it do to worry anyway? It sure doesn't make
you live longer. It won't make you taller."

Pete laughed. The guys gave Tom a hard time about
being the short man on the team, but Tom didn't seem to
mind.

"All right. So we won't starve," Tom conceded. "But
you can't stand in front of Columbus politicians dressed like
that."

Again came the infectious laughter, and Josh pointed
out Pete's window. "Look at those flowers! How could you
see that Queen Anne's lace, that sugar clover, the black-eyed
Susans out in the field, that purple bellflower there, even the
dandelions—and still worry about what kind of clothes
we're going to wear? Those wildflowers are more beautiful

Dandi Daley Mackall

than any clothes ever worn on earth! Do you think God's going to take such great care of flowers, which are here today and gone tomorrow, but forget about us? You have to have faith."

Maggie didn't say anything, but she took in every word. She'd worried about everything her whole life. It was worry about the future that had made her give in to her mother's demand that she go through with the abortion. It was worry that kept her from getting closer to Josh's followers. She didn't want them to find out about her past. She was worried what they'd think of her. Besides, if there were an award for the worst-dressed person in the group, Maggie knew she'd win, no contest. Krystal showed up in new clothes every time she joined them. Maggie wore the same things day in and day out.

But listening to Josh made her want to let go of every single worry.

"So," Josh concluded, "do we have a deal? No more worrying about food or clothes or anything else? Let the rest of the world worry about that. Your Father knows what you need better than you do, and he'll give you everything you need from day to day, if you live for him. Don't sweat tomorrow. Tomorrow will take care of itself."

❖

Gradually, the roadside grew less green, and traffic thickened. Pete slowed to let the RV catch up, then took the 9th Street exit. They passed Jacob's Field and kept going until they turned onto 116th. Maggie wondered if Matt, driving the RV, was feeling what she was feeling. This was their old territory. She didn't like the memories that sprang up, like the biography of another Maggie, still there, not quite dead. She remembered driving here in the wee hours by herself because she couldn't make it until the morning without a hit.

Maggie believed what Josh had told them about living a new life. She just couldn't understand why so much of the old garbage still hung out in the dark corners of her mind. She wanted to ask Josh why that life couldn't just stay dead forever. But she still wasn't as comfortable talking to Josh as the others seemed to be. She had the strong urge to lock the doors of the pickup, as if that could keep everything bad out.

Josh directed them to an even rougher-looking neighborhood, around 130th and Union. Boarded-up shops and tenement buildings with plywood windows were scattered across vacant lots. People stood around, waiting. There were beer-drinking gangs with rival tattoos, old people carrying brown bags, families with kids. Groups of people littered the streets. Others lay in the dirt next to a chain-link fence.

This was how Maggie had pictured her life if she'd gone through with her pregnancy, if she'd had Chance. On her own, without even a high school diploma, she'd figured that this was where she would have ended up.

"They're not going to riot or anything, are they?" Tom asked.

Maggie guessed that it was at least 90 degrees out there. She couldn't help wondering what would happen to their whole group if the crowd turned mean. People here had seen what happened in the LA riots. They'd had their own.

"Tom," Josh said patiently, "nice to know the pep talk on worry really soaked in."

Maggie grinned. She'd been worried too. It was amazing how easy it was to forget some things, and how impossible to forget others.

The street ended in a wide, barren acreage that might have been a park in another lifetime. Now the only things there were weeds and broken glass. People milled around the dirt lot. Some sat on blankets, as if they were having a picnic or waiting for a concert.

"Drive over the curb and up to that tree." Josh pointed to a scrawny tree in the center of the lot.

Pete did it, waiting for people to move out of the way. He shut off the engine, and they climbed out of the truck. Behind them, Matt stopped at the curb, and the others piled out of the RV and followed them on foot.

Jude began setting up the sound system from the truck bed, while Josh made his way through the crowd, shaking hands and returning hugs. People wanted to be near him, to touch him.

But there were others who didn't act like fans. They hooted from the backs of cars and yelled obscenities from the tops of buildings.

"How about doing that water-to-champagne jazz, dude?" a guy yelled from the back of a jeep.

Women leaned out from tenement windows to watch the spectacle. Kids played on fire escapes. Maggie spotted Andy helping an old woman sit down on a tiny patch of green in the only shade around. A herd of spectators thundered by, nearly knocking Andy over. Matt and Pete helped maneuver a man in a wheelchair over the dusty, bumpy lot.

A group of little kids, screaming and laughing, raced up to the truck. Maggie couldn't take her eyes off them. She knew she should be looking for ways to help the crowd, like Matt and the others were. But she couldn't stop thinking of how things might have turned out if she hadn't gotten into the car with her mother that day. If she hadn't gotten out of the car at the clinic. If she'd kept Chance.

Jude hopped down from the pickup and blocked the kids from climbing into the truck and mobbing Josh, who was now in the bed of the pickup getting ready to speak. "Hey! Get out of here! Don't touch this equipment!"

Pete ran up to help. He stood next to Jude and yelled for the parents to come and get their kids.

Maggie couldn't stop watching a little boy about the age Chance would have been. Matt came running up and stopped in front of the boy. "Don't bother Joshua, kiddo!" he warned.

The boy's eyes widened in fear. His sides heaved. His lips quivered.

Maggie couldn't stand it. Before she even realized what she was doing, she threw herself between Matt and the boy. "Leave this boy alone!"

"Maggie!" Jude shouted. "Those kids can't be here. Josh is going to talk in just a minute. The kids will be in the way."

Maggie started to protest, but Josh beat her to it. He jumped from the truck and stretched out his arms to all the children. "Come on up here, guys!"

Kids raced into his arms, knocking him backward onto the ground. Josh laughed as the boy Maggie had been watching climbed on top of him. The others piled on, acting like Josh was their long-lost father. When he sat up again, the children climbed into his lap. They overflowed and held on to him, hugging him.

Maggie imagined Chance there in the middle of the scene. How incredible it would have been to have the two of them together! She knew she had never loved Josh more than at this moment. She loved him in the way she'd wanted to love God when she was a child, with everything good that was in her, with her whole heart and mind and soul.

Josh turned to Matt and the others. "Don't ever stop children from coming to me. The kingdom of God belongs to children just like these!"

The little boy Maggie had watched squealed. Maggie laughed out loud.

Josh turned to the crowd. "Listen to me! Look at these kids! Anyone who doesn't have a childlike faith, a trust like these kids have, won't ever get into heaven." He hugged each of the children individually and whispered something in each child's ear before sending them all back to sit with their parents or grandparents. "Take good care of your children," Josh warned them, "or you'll have your Father in heaven to answer to."

Maggie stopped laughing.

Josh leaped back into the truck bed and stood in front of the mike in his jeans and T-shirt. His gaze moved across the crowd. It had grown, with people spread over rooftops and into alleys. They overflowed into streets as far as Maggie could see. There were thousands and thousands gathered in this inner-city wasteland, waiting for Josh.

"Lay it on us!" someone shouted.

"Peace, man!"

"Love, baby!"

Josh began quietly. "Love God with all your heart, mind, and soul. And love your neighbor like you love yourself."

The crowd grew quiet, even the hecklers. Maggie thought this was another miracle in itself. Then one of them hollered out, "Yeah? So who's my neighbor?" The guy was rewarded with a ripple of laughter.

"Once upon a time," Josh began, ignoring the smart-aleck groans from the hecklers, "a gang attacked a homeless man on a backstreet in Cleveland. The poor guy didn't have much, but they took the change in his pocket. Then they kicked him and beat him just for the sport of it, and left him for dead. A little while later, a Worship House leader passed by on his way to a service. He saw the groaning homeless man, but he couldn't stop because he didn't want to keep his congregation waiting.

"A few hours later, a Community Hall leader was out for her daily run. She took one look at the homeless man and jogged across the street, thinking the bum was no doubt getting what he deserved. Then a high school punk, a gang member from the hood, came strutting by. When he saw the homeless man, he stopped. A rush of pity, or compassion, came over him. He felt the man's pulse and saw that he was alive. So he picked up the man and carried him fourteen blocks to the free clinic. He stayed with the man until the doctor came. Then he watched as they bandaged the man. "'If you need money to keep him here,'" the guy said, handing over all the cash he had on him, "'take this. I can get more. I'll come back and pay you whatever he owes you, okay?'"

Josh stopped talking.

Maggie gazed at the crowd. No one was heckling now. Everyone waited for the ending. The boy Chance's age snuggled up to a woman who could have been his grandmother.

"So," Josh continued, staring down the heckler who had asked the question, "which of these three would you say was a neighbor to the man who was attacked?"

The same guy, not a heckler anymore, answered, "The one who helped him!"

"Right on!" Josh said.

The crowd broke into applause. Josh waved it off and launched into story after story. Between the stories, people came to the truck to be healed. The man in the wheelchair walked. Old people, teens, and babies were brought to Josh, and he never got tired of making them well.

Then he started telling stories again, and the crowd settled in as the day passed and the evening came. Josh talked all night, and nobody left. In fact, more and more came.

Maggie spotted a group of men who looked like Worship House leaders. No way did they come from this neighborhood. One of them called out to Josh, "Why are you down here in the slums, talking to these . . . these gangs? You're wasting your time on people like this!"

Pete started toward the man, but Josh stopped him. He didn't answer the leader, at least not directly. "I've got another story for you."

The kids cheered, then quieted down.

"A man who had worked hard his whole life to build up a small chain of grocery stores had two sons. He'd always expected them to carry on the business and had drawn up his will, leaving them everything.

"But that wasn't good enough for the younger son. So one day he walked into the shop and told his dad, 'I want my share of everything now, while I'm young enough to enjoy it.' His father didn't like the idea, of course, but he saw that this was what his son wanted. So he divided his money between his sons right there.

"A few days later," Josh continued to the silent crowd, "the younger son packed his bags and flew to California. He bought a place in Hollywood, and before long it was the place to party—drugs, women, everything he thought he'd always wanted. But when the house emptied, when he was all alone, there was nothing left inside of him."

Maggie had been standing beside the truck for hours. Now, as she remembered that feeling Josh was talking about—the total emptiness—she slid to the ground. Matt walked over and sat beside her. She knew he understood. He'd felt it too. Matt pointed to a break between tenement houses, where the first hint of sunrise pressed up from the dirt and weeds.

"Even before the money was all gone and the bill collectors started calling," Josh continued, "before the bank foreclosed on the house and he ended up on the streets, the boy felt a cold desperation. He was alone, and he had no idea what to do. First he asked the people who had come to his parties if they could put him up, but they didn't want anything to do with him now. He tried sleeping on the beach, but he was arrested for vagrancy. He got so hungry that he begged people on the streets for spare change."

This was another version of the way Maggie had imagined her life with Chance. While she'd sat in the waiting room of the abortion clinic, she'd told herself that she was doing the best thing for everybody. Alan didn't want a child. Maggie's mother didn't want the embarrassment of an illegitimate baby around. Maggie would have been on her own. She might have had to beg on the streets, just like the younger son in this story. Or worse. What kind of life would that have been for Chance?

Josh's voice had lowered. He didn't need to shout because everybody was listening intently. "Then one night as the younger son was digging through a filthy Dumpster behind a fast-food joint, he fell in. He lay there, covered in stinking grease and garbage. A rat crawled over his ankle. He screamed and kicked it off. Garbage flew over him. He brushed it off wildly.

"And that's when it struck him. Back home, even the bag boys, even the janitors who cleaned his father's stores, had food to eat and plenty of it. And here he was, in a Dumpster, dying of hunger. He determined to get back home however he could and tell his father how sorry he was. He'd beg him for any job he could get.

"It wasn't easy, but he made it back to Cleveland. It was early in the morning when he turned onto his street, long before the time his father always unlocked the grocery store.

"But—" Josh paused, and Maggie could see everybody lean in, waiting for the ending—"while the son was still at the far end of the street, his father saw him coming. Filled with love and compassion, the father ran down the street and hugged the boy, kissing him over and over.

"'Father,' said the son, 'I'm so sorry. I've wasted everything. I've done terrible things. You shouldn't even let me in the house or call me your son anymore.' But his dad shouted, waking the whole neighborhood, 'Everybody come here! My son is back! We're going to celebrate!' He got the best steaks and ribs in the market, together with all the fixings, and cooked up the biggest barbeque anyone had ever seen around there.

"Then the older brother drove up. He'd been managing the branch store and checking on the day's deliveries in East Cleveland. When he saw the crowd and the cookout in front of his father's store, he stopped and asked one of the checkout girls what was going on. 'Your little brother's back!' she explained. 'And your dad's so psyched that he's almost emptied out the whole store to celebrate.'

"The brother couldn't believe it. He was so angry that he stormed around outside until his dad came over to him and begged him to come and eat with them. '*I'm* the one who's slaved around here for you!' the elder son protested. 'I've done everything! Now my good-for-nothing brother comes back, and you throw him a party? When did I ever get a party?' His dad tried to make him understand. 'Son, you and I are close. Everything I have is yours. But we had to celebrate your brother coming home. It's like he was dead, and now he's come back to life! We lost him, but now we've found him again."

Maggie glanced back at the Worship House leader, the one who had asked Josh why he was wasting time with these people. She knew the story was a direct hit. The leaders were like the older brother, who kept all the rules. And then Josh had come along and welcomed people like Maggie and Matt to come to his Father—not just the rule keepers.

"There they go," Matt said as the group of leaders stormed off. "Guess they got the point."

Matt was laughing, but something in Maggie wasn't laughing. The Worship House leaders had a lot of power, just like the governor and Senator Harold. The more people who followed Josh, the more the leaders were going to resent him. But Josh wasn't doing anything to gain their approval. In fact, everywhere they went, they seemed to tick off more and more leaders and politicians.

Maggie wondered if Josh knew how dangerous it could be to offend the wrong people.

Chapter Fifteen

Josh kept healing people and telling stories. Nobody had eaten anything since the day before. Finally, late in the day, Tom came to where Maggie and Matt were sitting. "We've got to do something," he whispered. "Josh needs to send people home so they can get something to eat. I've been talking with the others. They all agree."

Maggie was pretty hungry herself, and she couldn't remember seeing so much as a McDonald's or a 7-Eleven anywhere around. She and Matt walked over to the pickup with Tom. Pete, Andy, and a few of the others were already there.

Pete was shouting up at Josh, who was listening to a talkative elderly man. "Josh, you need to send everybody home. It's really hot. Nobody's had anything to eat. They're going to start getting sick."

"Pete's right," Andy chimed in. "We've asked, and there's nothing to eat around here."

Josh didn't look the least bit worried. "Well, *you* feed them."

"Right," Tom muttered.

"Come on," Josh coaxed. "You're a resourceful group."

Matt stammered, "You're . . . you're not serious. It would take a fortune to feed these people!"

"And we don't have that kind of money!" Jude added.

Josh sighed, but that twinkle was there in his eyes. "How much food *do* we have?"

Pete shrugged.

"Well, go find out," Josh urged.

The boy Maggie had been watching all day was sitting on his grandmother's lap, tugging at her shirt to get her attention. "Gram!" he said. "We have a peanut-butter sandwich."

When Andy glanced over at the little boy, Maggie figured he must have heard too.

"Well, Josh," Andy said, "the little boy there has a peanut-butter sandwich. That's not going to go very far." He gazed around at the crowd. "Not with, what, maybe a hundred thousand or more?"

"Perfect!" Josh exclaimed. "Matt?" He motioned for

Matt to collect the sandwich. Then he told Andy and Pete and the others to have everybody sit in groups of about fifty.

The boy beamed as he handed the wrapped peanut-butter-on-white-bread sandwich to Matt. Matt brought it back to Josh. An old woman ambled over to Maggie and handed her a package of paper plates. Maggie thanked her and ran the plates up to Josh. She watched as he broke the sandwich into pieces and put the pieces onto the first plate.

Maggie saw him do it. The plate was filled. But when Tom took it and Matt held out another plate, Josh kept breaking off pieces of that peanut-butter sandwich until the second plate was full too. Brad filed by next and had his plate filled. Then Jessica, Krystal, Jude, Andy, and so on, until every paper plate was piled high with pieces of the boy's sandwich. Maggie knew she should go to Josh too. She could get a plate and watch him fill it with food for the crowd.

But she couldn't. Her mouth felt dry, as if she'd eaten peanut butter that stuck in her throat. Instead of helping in the miracle, she watched tiny hands reach for pieces of sandwich. There were fistfuls of food for every child.

Josh was meeting all of the people's needs. Maggie knew that many of the mothers she saw smiling across the lot must have been single moms raising kids on their own. Only that was just it. They weren't alone. Their children weren't starving. Josh was taking care of each one.

Josh would have taken care of Chance.

❖

Dear Chance,

I saw a miracle today. Josh fed a crowd of thousands with nothing but a peanut-butter sandwich. I would have given anything to have you there to see it.

People laughed as they passed the food around. Even Krystal got into it. I saw her eating with a group of gang girls she wouldn't have been caught dead with in the high school cafeteria.

When everyone was done, the guys collected left-overs—12 plates stacked high with food. Josh gave the food to the women around him to share with anybody who needed it. He had Jude give them all of the money we had left in our account, too.

It was dark as we loaded the truck and the RV. Somebody cried out, "Joshua Davidson for president!" That's when Josh turned to us and said, "We need to leave now." Jude tried to argue, but Josh insisted. As we drove away, people were chanting, "Josh for pres!" Headlights flashed. Horns blared.

You and I could have been in that crowd together, Chance. I didn't know Josh wouldn't let us starve. I was afraid we would end up like some of the mothers and sons I saw today. But do you know what? They're fine. They're more than fine. I saw love there. And happiness. I'm sure there must have been sadness there, too. But that's everywhere.

We would have been all right—you and me. With Josh, we could have had it all.

Chapter Sixteen

The day after Josh's visit to inner-city Cleveland, the Cleveland *Plain Dealer* published a front-page feature on the event. The headline read "Peanut-Butter Miracle."

Maggie had picked up a paper while they were visiting Medina Hospital, but she didn't get a chance to read it until that evening, when they set up camp. The newspaper piece explained the "sandwich phenomenon" as an event of mass generosity, with people deciding to share their lunches. Much of the article was dedicated to Josh's supposed bid for the presidential primary. It said that seven states, including Ohio, were considering putting Josh on the ballot.

Maggie thought about the chant that had coursed through the city of Cleveland as they'd driven away: "Josh for president! Josh for president!" She wondered if Josh had talked to Pete or Brad about running. She'd never been the least bit interested in politics. But if Josh ran, she'd campaign for him.

Maggie spotted Josh stacking wood. She walked over and picked up sticks for kindling. "Josh," she asked, dumping the sticks into a pile, "are you thinking about running for president?"

Josh laughed, but Maggie didn't feel that he was laughing at her for asking. She believed she could ask Josh anything. "I'm afraid people only want me for president because they like what I give them, like the food yesterday. I wish people would yearn the same way for spiritual things."

Maggie nodded. It wasn't until later that she realized he hadn't exactly said yes or no to running for president.

The rest of the night, Maggie watched the stars poke through the sky. She spread out one of the sleeping bags in a corner of the truck bed, sat, and stared up, trying to pick out constellations. She could still recognize the Big and Little Dippers, and she was reasonably sure she made out Orion's Belt.

Krystal walked over to the truck. "Maggie, you're not going to sleep outside again, are you? Why don't you come sleep in the RV? We're making popcorn."

Maggie smiled at her. She knew Krystal was trying to

be friendly. She'd already apologized a dozen times for having been a brat to Maggie in school. Maggie knew she should say yes, but she needed to be outside, to sleep under the stars, at least one more night. "Maybe next time. Thanks, though."

Krystal sighed. "Okay. But if you change your mind or get cold or anything, the offer still stands."

Once she was by herself again, Maggie grabbed an extra blanket and curled up. She'd just dozed off when she heard tapping. Someone was knocking on the tailgate of the pickup. Maggie sat up and saw Brad and Bob.

"Mind if we join you, Maggie?" Bob asked.

"We can leave, if you want to be alone," Brad added quickly.

Bob nodded back at the RV. "Krystal dragged out her games again. I can't take another round of Monopoly."

Maggie grinned and motioned for them to climb in. She knew what people were saying about "Josh's women." She'd seen the stupid things people wrote on the Internet. Tom had shown her an editorial that called Josh and his followers "modern-day hippies." One of the talk-show psychologists had done a whole show on Josh, without even asking him to appear. They made the group out to be a dangerous cult and insinuated that the men seduced young women to join. There were rumors about drugs and orgies.

The boys grabbed a couple of blankets and sat crammed in next to her. For a while, they sat there in silence, gazing at the stars.

Maggie smiled to herself. Here she was, in the back of a pickup with two men, and she wasn't a bit worried about anything happening, about either of them taking advantage of her. It hadn't been easy for Maggie to join a group with so many men involved. She'd known too many men in her lifetime. One way or another, they'd all ended up using her. Her father. Alan. Ben. She didn't think Alan had set out to hurt her any more than she'd meant to hurt him. But he had.

The last time Maggie had seen Alan, Chance's father, he'd come by her apartment. It had been her twenty-first birthday, and Chance would have been three years old. Maggie hadn't seen Alan since he'd left for Kent State. His parents had moved somewhere down south, so he had no reason to come back to Slayton—and at least one good reason not to.

She'd seen him there by chance. That's how she'd thought of it . . . in those exact words: *by chance.* He was walking out of the First Federal Bank on Main Street. He saw her a second after she'd spotted him. He hadn't changed much. Same thick, brown hair, falling carelessly over his broad forehead. He hadn't even filled out much, the way a lot of his old classmates had. Alan still looked like a boy.

Maggie had made the first move, glad that she'd decided to dress up and get her hair styled on her birthday as a gift to herself.

Her only birthday gift, as it turned out.

"Hey, Alan. Welcome back."

"Maggie?" Alan had actually sounded pleased to see her. He'd hurried down the bank steps to meet her. The sun was shining, with only a few clouds floating in the sky.

Maggie had managed to smile back at him. "Alan. It's been a long time."

"You look great!" He eyed her up and down, his gaze lingering at her breasts. "What are you up to these days?"

Maggie had just gotten "promoted" from janitor to bartender/waitress at the bar, so she told him that. He told her about Kent State. He'd been there three years and still didn't know what to major in, but he'd gotten into a top fraternity.

Maggie couldn't remember if she'd asked him to see her new apartment, or if that had been his idea. But that's where they ended up. They had a drink together, for old time's sake, and then another. And another. They'd started with wine and ended with Jack Daniel's.

They'd made love on the living-room floor. No, even then, Maggie had known that what they were doing had nothing to do with love. For her, it had been a desperate attempt to fill the hole inside her. For Alan, it must have been fun—at least until it was over.

Maggie had broken down then, fallen apart. "We killed him," she'd muttered over and over again, sitting on the floor, snot running down her face as she cried uncontrollably. "We killed our son."

Alan had backed away from her and pulled his clothes on so fast, he'd almost toppled over. "Stop it!" he'd shouted. "Stop saying that. It wasn't a son, and you don't know *whose* it was!" Even now, Maggie remembered Alan's face closing over and shutting her out for good. "Look at yourself, Maggie. You're a slut now. And you were a slut then. What did you expect?"

She hadn't been able to answer him. She hadn't been able to speak.

He'd walked out without looking back, and she hadn't seen him since.

Her life had shattered into tiny pieces that wouldn't fit back together, that hadn't fit back together, until she'd found Josh.

A cell phone rang, startling her out of the past.

It rang until Bob gave in and answered it. "Yes, Mother. No. No, we won't be home then. . . . I know. . . . Well, tell Dad we're sorry. . . . At least a week, I guess." There was a long, long silence then, during which Bob and Brad made faces at each other. "Don't you want to talk to Brad?" Bob asked, smirking at his brother.

Brad waved his arms in protest, then put his head on his folded hands, as if he were sleeping.

"All right," Bob said into the phone. "I'll tell him." He clicked off the cell. "Brad, your mother says shame on you for not calling her."

Sally, the boys' mother, was quite a woman. When Bob and Brad were in school, Sally had been president of the PTA more times than anyone else in the history of the school. She'd headed up most of the committees, too, from Founders Day to homecoming. Sally had shown up for several of Josh's events, and she always sent casseroles and pies with the boys.

Josh's mother did the same thing, showing up now and then, and never empty-handed. But Mrs. Davidson wasn't like Sally. There was a completely different spirit about Josh's mother. Maggie loved it when she showed up. She always greeted Maggie like a friend, like a niece or a daughter. Mrs. Davidson's life hadn't been easy, but she had a joy, a gentle spirit about her that made people want to be around her. Maggie hoped that one day she'd have a chance to really get to know the woman.

Maggie gave up on getting any sleep for a while. "How's your dad getting along without you guys at the cycle shop?"

"Dad's had to scale down," Brad answered.

"Mom's been helping out in sales a couple days a week, besides keeping the company books," Bob added.

Maggie grinned. "I'll bet your mother is a great saleswoman. Who could say no to her?"

They laughed.

Maggie leaned back and gazed up at the starry sky. "Brad, read the psalm about the stars. Please?" She'd been reading the Scriptures Andy had given her, and she loved the psalms.

"Which one, Maggie?"

"The one about the work of God's fingers."

Brad didn't even have to dig out his Scriptures. He had so much of it memorized. "'O Lord, our Lord, your majestic name fills the earth! Your glory is higher than the heavens. You have taught children and infants to tell of your strength. . . .'"

Maggie had forgotten that part—about the children and infants. She shut her eyes and hoped the darkness hid her face.

Brad kept reciting the psalm: "'When I look at the night sky and see the work of your fingers—the moon and the stars you set in place—what are people that you should think of them, mere mortals that you should care for them?'"

Maggie fell asleep under the stars, listening to the words . . . and dreaming of Chance.

※

Maggie didn't wake up until someone tossed a sleeping bag into the truck bed. She couldn't believe she'd slept so long. Brad and Bob were gone. Everyone else was up and busy. She smelled bacon and sat up fast, brushing her hair out of her face.

"Morning, sleepyhead!" Matt called. He was carrying water to a grill. Sally was there again, standing over the cookstove, cooking bacon and eggs. Maggie smelled fresh coffee. Sally must have come at dawn.

They ate a great breakfast together. Maggie had become convinced that everything tastes better when cooked and eaten outside in the chill of the morning. They didn't camp all the time, but she loved it when they did. Before traveling with Josh, she'd rarely eaten breakfast. And she'd never camped out.

"We'll be heading for Columbus before long," Josh said when they were almost finished. "You all know that, right? And you know that the religious and political leaders there aren't going to like me. They'll hate me, in fact, and they'll hate you too. You need to start getting ready for Columbus."

Maggie didn't understand why Josh said things like that. Every now and then he'd bring up Columbus, and his whole mood would change. She wasn't the only one who didn't want to talk about it either. Whenever Josh started

Dandi Daley Mackall

talking about the bad things that were coming, one of them would change the subject—fast.

This time it was Matt. "So, are we going to Cincinnati this week?" he asked, taking another cup of coffee from Sally's fresh pot.

But Josh couldn't be thrown off. "You need to hear me," he continued, ignoring Matt's question. "I know you can't handle what's coming yet. But I have to start getting you ready. They're going to kill me."

Maggie couldn't breathe. *Kill him? Kill Josh?* He couldn't be serious.

Before anybody could react, Josh added quickly, "But I'll be raised up again after three days."

Pete was on his feet so fast, his coffee spilled. "Don't even talk like that, Josh! We'd never let that happen!"

Josh turned on Pete. "Stop it! Just stop it! Whose side are you on, Pete? You're not seeing things the way God the Father does. You're just looking at your own little world." Josh studied the rest of them sitting around the morning fire. "If you want to be my followers, you have to stop being selfish. Stop trying to get the things everybody wants down here. If you try to hang on to your life for yourself, you'll lose it. But if you give up your life for me, you'll find real life."

Nobody had a comeback.

Sally broke the awkward silence by refilling everybody's coffee cup. Maggie tried to put Josh's warning out of her head. She wouldn't want to live if they killed Josh. There would be nothing to live for.

Sally finished packing up the dishes, and people wandered off to their cars. The rest of them would split up between the RV and the pickup. As usual, Bob and Brad made a dash for the front seat of the RV.

"Wait just a minute!" Matt shouted. "This isn't fair. Why do you two always get the front seat?"

"We called it!" Bob yelled back, one hand on the door.

Maggie thought they sounded like two-year-olds.

Josh stood to the side, watching them.

Then Sally walked up. "Joshua," she began, her eyes cast down respectfully, "I've been wanting to ask you a favor. Now seems as good a time as any."

When Bob and Brad hurried back to stand by their mother, Maggie got the feeling that whatever was going on, the Sons of Thunder were in on it.

Josh smiled down at her. "What is it, Sally?"

"In the New World you're building, will you let my two sons be leaders? Maybe vice presidents? Or your chief advisors?"

Maggie heard grumbling from Jude, Tom, and the others. She cringed inside, amazed that Sally would have the nerve to ask this in front of everybody. But she understood, in a way. Sally would do anything for her boys. Maggie would have been the same way for Chance.

Josh sighed deeply and closed his eyes for a second. "Sally, you don't have any idea what you're asking. Do you think they're able to go through what I'm about to go through?"

"We are!" Bob shouted.

"We really are," Brad agreed.

Josh stared at them for a long time before answering. When he did, he sounded sad. "I'm afraid you're right. You

Dandi Daley Mackall

are going to have to go through a lot. But it's not up to me who my right-hand men in heaven will be. My Father makes those decisions."

"I don't know who you guys think you are," Andy complained.

"You got that right!" Pete seconded.

Thad, another follower, looked indignant. "I've had twenty years' experience running major companies. What have you boys done? Sold a few motorcycles?"

Matt and Krystal were arguing, and Tom tried to shout something at both of them.

"Stop it," Josh said. "This is exactly how the world works. Didn't your bosses lord it over you? Haven't you hated the way people with power treat the people under them? You can't be like that! Anyone who wants to be a leader here should be a servant. Look at me! Did I come here so I could be served by you or by anybody? No! I came to serve, to give up my life for you."

Josh turned to Sally, who hadn't moved since she'd asked her question and started the whole argument. "Does this answer your question, Sally?" Then he walked away.

If Maggie had been Sally, she would have crawled under a rock and never come out.

Chapter Seventeen

Thunder rumbled in the distance. They were the only campers still in the park.

Josh didn't seem to notice the sudden change in the weather. "Go on ahead to Cincinnati. I need some time to myself."

Pete tossed Josh the keys to the truck. "Okay. We'll meet you there. You can take the truck."

Josh tossed the keys back to Pete. "No. You take the truck *and* the RV."

Pete caught the keys. "How are *you* going to get there?"

Josh smiled at him. "Don't worry about it, Pete. Go!" He glanced at the sky, where the gray clouds were turning darker and growing, eating up the white and blue like hungry monsters. Then he ran up the hill and out of sight.

"We can't just leave him here," Tom objected.

"That's what he wants." Brad put his hand on Tom's back and urged him toward the RV. Most of the others followed.

Maggie saw a streak of lightning. Then thunder followed. She waited for the old storm panic to hit her, but it didn't.

"Maggie!" Krystal yelled back. "You better come in the RV with us. It looks like a bad storm's on the way."

Maggie waved at her. "Thanks, Krystal! I'm fine!" It was true. For the first time in years, Maggie was in a storm and she wasn't afraid. She would have ridden in the back of the truck if Pete and Andy hadn't made her come into the cab with them.

When Pete eased onto the highway, windshield wipers swishing, the road was already covered with water. Headlights were swallowed in the fog. Rain drummed the roof of the truck. Maggie sat by the window, where she could gaze at the sky and watch the clouds open and pour down rain.

They stayed on I-71 south past Ashland and Mansfield. The rain never let up. They'd been on the road over an hour when Pete slammed on his brakes. Maggie gripped the dashboard. Matt had to pull the RV into the left lane to keep from ramming them from behind.

"Pete!" Andy cried.

"Did you see him?" Pete whispered.

"See who?" Andy demanded.

Maggie tried to peer out Pete's window, but the rain was still coming down, blurring the window glass. The RV had pulled over in front of them, emergency lights flashing. There were no other cars on the road.

"I saw Josh," Pete said. He'd stopped the truck in the middle of the road and made no attempt to pull it over. Pete stared at his hands, still clenching the steering wheel, as if he were afraid to look outside.

"Pete, that's crazy!" Andy started to laugh but couldn't pull it off. "Do you want me to drive awhile?"

Maggie thought she saw something—*someone*—walking toward them. "Pete, roll down the window!"

The figure came closer. Arms waved at them.

Then she saw his smile. There was no mistaking who it was. "Josh!"

Andy gasped.

The door of the RV swung open, and Matt rushed outside. Bob and Brad followed him. Then the others. Maggie ran outside too, laughing out loud. It couldn't be Josh. They'd left him at the park. Yet here he was, standing with them. And even though rain still slashed from the sky in a deluge, Josh was completely dry.

Impossible.

The thought made her laugh louder than the wind. *Impossible.* As if there were such a thing!

Josh scruffed the heads of the Sons of Thunder, gave them his biggest grin, then walked to the truck. He climbed into the backseat and fell instantly asleep. They all followed at a safe distance, then stared in at him through the truck window.

After a few minutes, they got back into the vehicles and headed out, with Pete taking the lead again.

Pete squinted through the rain-streaked windshield, while Andy and Maggie stared at the road. They rode in silence. Maggie wasn't sure if they were quiet so they wouldn't wake Josh in the backseat, or if they simply didn't know what to say.

Suddenly the rain stopped—just like that. The sky turned yellow. The wind, which earlier had blown strong enough to shake the truck, now felt unearthly still.

Maggie rolled down the window and breathed in. The air smelled wrong—not like storm air but something worse. The eerie yellow light made it feel as if time had gotten stuck somewhere between day and night.

A cell phone rang.

Maggie jumped.

Andy got it. "Yeah?" He listened, then turned to Pete. "It's Matt. He says there are tornado warnings out. One's been sighted pretty close to here."

Pete craned his neck, trying to see up in the sky. "Must be why nobody's on the road. What's Matt think we should do?"

"That's why he's calling us." Andy put his ear back to the phone. "Just hang on a minute, Matt."

Lightning cracked, splitting the sky in two. Maggie told herself she wouldn't be afraid. But this wasn't just a storm. "Maybe you should pull over, Pete." She thought that's what you were supposed to do in case you got caught outside during a tornado. Maybe lie in a ditch. She couldn't remember for sure. She couldn't think straight.

Pete slowed the truck and pulled over on the side of the road. The RV drove up close behind them and honked.

Maggie glanced back at Josh, who was still sleeping peacefully.

"Do something, Pete!" Andy had to shout, because the wind howled so loud they could barely hear each other. It sounded like a train was headed for them.

A scream came over Andy's cell, so loud Maggie could hear it. It was Krystal. She was screaming something, but Maggie couldn't understand. Then she got it. "It's a tornado!" Krystal was crying. "Right there!"

Maggie stuck her head out the window. A white funnel cloud, still a distance away, was heading straight for them. The tail swept the highway in front of them. She screamed too.

Bob and Brad ran from the RV toward them, but they had to fight the wind to get there. They pounded on Pete's door, and he fumbled to roll down the window.

"Where's Josh?" Brad cried. He hung on to the door handle while Bob held on to him.

With a kind of surreal fascination, Maggie watched the funnel twist and spin up the road. She could see junk flying out from it, as if it were angry and throwing boards, wire, fences, and bushes at them.

This was it.

Maggie couldn't believe it was all going to end here.

What had happened to all of Josh's promises? Were they lies, like every other promise every other man had made to her? She should have known better.

"Wake him up!" Bob shouted.

Pete and Andy turned to the backseat. "Josh!" Pete called. "Get up! What's the matter with you? Don't you even care that we're going to die?"

"The tornado!" Andy cried. "It's here! It's coming right toward us!"

Maggie yelled too. She didn't even know what she was saying. Maybe she was just screaming at him.

Josh woke up and, without a word, stepped out of the truck and onto the highway. He strode toward the oncoming funnel, then stopped in the middle of the road, only a few feet from the truck. "Quiet!"

Josh spoke to the tornado, to the skies, but Maggie felt as if he had spoken to her. She watched as the funnel stopped spinning. It turned back into a cloud and was sucked up into a sky that instantly turned to midnight blue. The wind died down, and the stars filled the expanse above them, as if they'd been there all along. Maggie wasn't sure she'd ever seen so many stars.

Josh strolled back to them. "Why were you so afraid?" He stared from one to the other. He looked surprised that they'd been scared of a tornado. "Don't you have any faith in me at all?" Then he walked past them, back to the truck, and went back to sleep.

For minutes, Maggie and the others stood there on the highway, not saying a word.

Tom was the first to speak. "Who is he?"

It was a strange question, but Maggie bet every one of them was thinking the same thing.

She certainly was.

❖

Dear Chance,

Even tornadoes mind Josh.

You should have seen it. If CNN had captured that funnel cloud on tape, the moment Josh ordered that twister back to the sky, they would have run the pictures all day, instead of showing us pictures of the latest terrorist attack over and over. There was a terrible attack today in London and another threat on the Capitol Building in Columbus. All the state capitols are on high alert.

Back to the tornado. Chance, it was coming right at us. All I could think about was that my life was over and I hadn't done anything. I watched it come, and I was ready to believe that Josh was like every other man in my life who let me down.

He's right. I have so little faith in him.

Chapter Eighteen

Weeks passed, and Maggie was more amazed every day at the things Josh could do. He said they were heading for Columbus, but she understood now that he didn't mean geography. Somehow, whenever he talked about the things she didn't want him to, the warnings and predictions of things that would happen to him, he was saying that all those bad things were going to take place in Columbus. That's what he meant by "heading" there. His mind was set on whatever was coming.

They'd been circling the state, driving from Sandusky through Montpelier, down to Van Wert, over to Lima. In Dayton, a man who had been blind his whole life got his sight back. After that, wherever they went, people were waiting for them. Jude took pictures of the crowds, and a lot of the photos ended up in newspapers all across Ohio.

They visited the cancer unit in a hospital in Cincinnati. It was the children's ward, and Maggie's favorite day of their journey. Every child was cured by Josh. Kids jumped out of their beds, jumped *on* their beds. In one room, the parents and grandparents jumped on the hospital bed with their little girl. Maggie would have given anything to jump with them.

Sometimes Josh and his followers ate in hospital cafeterias. Other times, when Josh spoke in Worship Houses or Community Halls, they might get invited to someone's home for dinner or to a community supper. They'd buy groceries and cook in the RV or zip through a fast-food place. It didn't seem to matter, as long as they were together, with Josh.

Maggie still wasn't sure how she fit in exactly. One day she'd feel like Matt, Andy, Jessica, and the others were the family she'd always wanted. The next day she'd wonder why she was even along for the ride . . . why they bothered putting up with her. Then she'd slip away and write to Chance. When she came back, she was pretty sure nobody had even missed her.

Drugs had a way of creeping into her mind, sometimes for no reason. One morning, after they'd had a great night in Ashland, she'd been overwhelmed with the desire for a hit. She'd found Josh and talked to him for a while, and the urge had gone away. But it bothered her that she could still want it, even when things were going fine.

In Chillicothe, Ohio, when they were visiting a cardiac unit, Sally showed up. As soon as Josh saw her, he left what he was doing to give her a hug. From then on, Sally traveled with them through southern Ohio, and Maggie had to admit that she worked harder than any of them.

Sally had brought along enough money for everybody to spend a night in a little motel outside Portsmouth. Jessica's husband had cut her off from his bank accounts, and Krystal's husband had decided he'd contributed enough to his wife's "hobbies," so nobody had had money for hotel rooms in quite a while.

Maggie and Sally shared a room with Jessica and Krystal. The first thing Maggie did when they got to the room was call Samantha. It had been a week since she'd talked to her old friend.

Sam answered on the first ring. "Hello?"

Maggie could tell in that one word that Sam was doing great. "Sam, this is Maggie."

"Maggie! How are you? Where are you? The paper said you were in Dayton. Is everything okay? You're all right, aren't you?"

Maggie answered all the pertinent questions. "Sam, you should come with us. I miss you." She glanced over her shoulder to make sure the other women in the motel room weren't listening. She didn't want to hurt their feelings.

"I would love to, Maggie! But I'm totally sure I'm right where God wants me. We've started Scripture studies right here in town! Can you believe it?"

"Sam, that's so great!" Maggie wished she had half of Sam's courage. Here she was, traveling with Josh, in the middle of the action, and she hadn't done a fraction of the work for Josh that Sam was doing.

"It started with a couple of people in my apartment building," Sam explained. "One of them was a Community Hall leader for ten years, and her husband still is. She and Frank met Josh before I did. We started getting together three times a week to study the Scripture. Then we got more and more people and had to split off into smaller groups. It's spread all over town, Maggie! Almost everybody in Oberlin is studying the Scripture and seeing Josh in it."

They talked for a while, until Maggie's cell started cutting out. Then they signed off.

The women got candy bars and Diet Cokes from the vending machine, then turned on CNN. A leader from the Dayton Worship House was in a roundtable discussion about Josh, with the attorney general and the majority leader of the Ohio senate. Maggie was surprised how antagonistic they were toward Josh.

"They're just jealous," Sally snapped, shutting off the set.

The phone rang, and Krystal got it. "Hello?" She listened for a minute, then handed the receiver to Jessica. "It's your husband."

Jessica listened without saying anything except, "All right . . . okay . . . yes, I will." When she hung up, she smiled sadly at them. "I have to go home. My husband wants me to take the first plane out."

Maggie helped her throw her things together, and Sally

drove her to the airport. While they were gone, Maggie took a long, hot shower, then washed her clothes in the hotel laundry room. When she got back to the room, Sally had returned and had already washed her hair. Krystal was in the shower.

Maggie crawled under the covers, savoring the luxury of a thick mattress. "This is a wonderful gift, Sally." She scooched deeper under the covers. "Thank you so much for letting us do this. I almost feel guilty."

"Don't be silly," Sally answered. She sat on the bed, brushing her wet hair. "I felt guilty every day after I asked Josh that stupid favor for my boys. Take it from me. Guilt trips don't do a lick of good."

"Now, Sally—" Krystal came out of the bathroom, towel-drying her hair—"you and Josh have been all through this. It's over. Everybody understands."

"What counts is that *I* understand." Sally smiled and didn't look embarrassed, which is what Maggie knew she would have been, no matter how much time had passed. But Sally seemed different, softer somehow, from the day she'd left them at the campground. Maggie wondered what the woman had been going through since that morning.

Maggie wanted to make Sally feel better. "I'm sure Josh has totally forgiven you, Sally. That has to make you feel better. I mean, knowing he forgave me for—" she didn't want to get into all the things Josh had forgiven her for— "for everything, that's what made me want to follow him in the first place."

Sally nodded. "Of course Josh forgave me. I knew that the moment after I'd asked that silly question." She smiled at Maggie. "But now I've forgiven myself, Maggie. Isn't that something? As if it's not enough that Josh and the Father forgave me, he's taught me how to forgive myself."

Maggie stared at the older woman and knew that was it. That's what had changed in Sally. She'd forgiven herself. Of all the things Maggie had found to envy in the lives of the other women who traveled with them, this gift was the most enviable yet. Sally had forgiven herself.

Maggie marveled at it. What would that feel like, to forgive herself for Chance?

Sally asked them to fill her in on everything she'd missed in the weeks she'd been gone. Krystal and Maggie told her about feeding the crowds in Cleveland and about the tornado. Maggie did her best to describe the healings in every city. And Krystal retold all of Josh's stories, doing a pretty good job of imitating him.

Then Maggie starting thinking about the other things Josh had said, the things none of them liked to talk about. "Sally," she began, "have you ever been around when Josh talked about going to Columbus?"

"What do you mean?" Sally asked, climbing into the other double bed.

Maggie wasn't sure herself. "Sometimes Josh says things. Like that people there hate him and want to kill him. That they *will* kill him."

"Nonsense!" Sally exclaimed. "Who would want to kill that sweet man?"

Maggie shrugged. "The other night he said he was going to be betrayed."

Krystal folded down the rollaway and settled in. "Well,

that makes no sense. Didn't Pete or the other guys ask him what he meant?"

"Nope."

"Men," Krystal muttered.

"Well, I'll bet it was one of those stories of his, don't you?" Sally suggested, not sounding worried at all. "He probably said one thing but meant something else altogether."

Maggie liked that answer. She relaxed into it. Sally and Krystal were smarter than she was. If they weren't going to worry about it, neither would she.

"We better get some sleep." Krystal clicked off the light. "We have a big day at Kent State tomorrow. Night."

Kent State? Maggie never asked where they were going next. It didn't matter to her. But she'd never even considered they could end up at Kent. Kent State was the last place she wanted to go.

Alan was there.

Chapter Nineteen

It seemed to Maggie that her two roommates fell asleep as fast as the light went out. After an hour of tossing and turning, she got up, carried her pack into the bathroom, took out paper and pen, and started a letter to Chance.

Dear Chance,
I'm trying hard to be a part of Josh's movement. I know from the outside I look like one of his followers. I'm following, after all, all over Ohio.

But am I really a part of what's happening? Or do I just have a front-row seat? Sometimes I wonder.

Tomorrow we're going to Kent State University. I don't know how I've managed to block the possibility of this out of my head, but I did. That's where Alan, your dad, goes, or went. I don't even know which. But I think he's still there. And I don't want to run into him. I know I should want him to be there to hear Josh. But I don't. I don't know what I'll do if I see him again.

❧

The next morning they drove to Kent, the site of Kent State University. Matt, Krystal, and most of the others strolled through the campus, inviting students to come and hear Josh speak. Maggie hung back with Jude and helped with the sound equipment.

The Student Center University Plaza was already filling with students. They sat on blankets and towels. Some had dragged out folding chairs. Maggie couldn't help scanning the crowd, looking for Alan. Hoping not to see him. Hoping to see him.

By the time Josh started speaking, the plaza was crammed. From the beginning, Josh captivated his audience. They listened while he talked about true knowledge and using their talents wisely. They laughed when he told them a story about the meanest man in the world dying and wanting to send back a message to his mean college-age son. After a while, Maggie almost forgot about Alan. She let herself drink in Josh's words, like everyone else there.

And then she saw him.

She heard Alan's voice before she turned to see him. She still knew his voice, after all this time. Her heart pounded as she slowly turned and looked behind her. He was smoking a cigarette, standing on the steps of the center. It was the same boyish Alan, only tanner, better dressed. He was with a thin, pretty blonde. His arm was draped across her shoulders, and hers wrapped about his waist. Maggie couldn't turn away. Her chest hurt, actually hurt, watching them. Yet she couldn't stop.

Alan took one last drag on his cigarette and dropped it. He stamped it out with his heel, a movement so familiar to her that she wanted to cry out to him. And then he looked up. He was facing in her direction. He was looking right at her.

Maggie didn't move. He squinted, his gaze squarely on her. She watched his lips twitch. She saw the fleeting smile. And then he turned his attention back to the girl.

Bile rose in Maggie's throat.

Had he even recognized her?

When she could move her body, she took off running, forcing her way through the crowd and back to the truck. She sat in the cab, alone, until it was over. And even when the others came back, when they piled into the truck and RV, when they drove to the next stop, filled with stories of what Josh had done, what he'd said, she was still alone.

❖

They left Athens and backtracked, instead of continuing to circle Ohio. Josh had Tom print out maps, with Columbus being the final destination. Everyone grew quiet. Maggie was afraid this was it, the time Josh had been talking about. But instead of going into the city, they turned off at a town called Harrisburg and stopped at the most beautiful house Maggie had ever seen. It looked like a transplanted Southern mansion.

A woman named Linda welcomed them. Maggie had never been in a home like this. It was the kind of house she'd dreamed of having right after she found out she was pregnant with Chance. That had been a pipe dream, but imagining a family and a house like this had helped her get through it.

Linda lived with her younger sister and older brother, Lawrence. Maggie took an immediate liking to Lawrence, who was old enough to be her father. And as he told her stories about when Joshua was a boy, she found herself wishing that she'd had a father like Lawrence. He and Josh went back a long ways.

Lawrence nodded toward his youngest sister, Beth, who was sitting on the floor, taking in every word Josh said. "Beth's been staring out the window all day, waiting for Josh."

Maggie understood. "She seems like a great kid." She hadn't meant to say "kid." Beth was probably close to Maggie's age. But her innocence made her seem younger.

"Linda and I couldn't get along without Beth, in more ways than one." Lawrence led Maggie to a greenhouse in back of the house.

Maggie stepped into a wonderland of flowers—roses, orchids, tropical flowers she'd never seen before. "They're amazing!"

"Beth makes a good living selling her flowers for banquets and weddings. I don't know what we'd do without the income, to be honest."

They had one of the best dinners Maggie could remember, followed by the best sleep she'd had in ages. Yet when she woke up, Maggie felt restless. Her skin crawled, and her head wouldn't stop buzzing. She wondered if the uneasiness was because she didn't belong in a home like this, or with people, families, like this. Wherever the restless, gnawing feeling came from, she wanted it to go away, because for the first time in weeks, Maggie felt like she needed something to take the edge off.

❖

Maggie was relieved that they didn't go on into Columbus. Instead they drove east, through Amish country, where they visited people who welcomed them to sleep in their barns for the night.

They kept mostly to out-of-the-way places on gravel roads and dirt lanes because Josh wanted to spend time alone with the group. About 70 or 80 followers met up with them in a campground outside of Youngstown. They hadn't camped for days, and Maggie had been looking forward to it.

Josh waited until they'd all finished Sally's great breakfast. Then he called them together. "It's your turn now." He glanced around the semicircle of followers. Most of them had been with him from the beginning. "Today I want you to go out and talk to the people. We'll meet back here tomorrow. Split up in pairs. Some of you can drive to

Youngstown. Others, head over to Wooster, or Akron and Canton—"

"Wait. Us?" Matt asked. "You're sending *us*?"

"What are *we* going to say?" Brad asked.

Josh smiled. "Tell people how much I love them. Talk to them about the Father. Help them understand why they need his forgiveness."

There were more questions, but Maggie didn't hear them or the answers, because she'd already decided she couldn't do it. There was no way she could talk to total strangers like that. How could she tell them what to do with their lives when she'd made such a mess of her own?

Tom had the most practical questions. "What should we take with us?"

"Nothing!" Josh grinned. "Just go! What's the worst that could happen?"

"They could tell us to get lost," a young woman from Akron suggested.

"Then do that," Josh replied. "And go somewhere else, to people who are ready to hear what you have to say."

Krystal actually looked excited about this. "Josh, where do you want us to stay overnight?"

"Stay with anyone who welcomes you into their home. You'll see. It will all work out. I'm giving you my strength and power to heal these people. And when you do, tell them how near the New World is to them."

They prayed together for a long time. Maggie could sense the awe around her. They were all ready, willing to trust Josh to use them like this. She was the only coward. Before the prayer ended, Maggie slipped away to the RV to write Chance.

Dear Chance,

I'm ashamed to write you that I'm the only follower here to stay behind. Seventy-two people have driven off to towns and cities to do what we've all been called by Josh to do. To tell others about him and about the Father's love for them. But here I am. I can't do it. After what I did to you, how can I tell anyone else what to do with his or her life? I have no right.

Maggie couldn't write any more. She folded the letter and put it into her pack, where she had dozens and dozens of Chance's letters. She had never reread them, but she always kept them with her.

Even after she heard everybody drive off, Maggie stayed inside the RV. She cleaned. She did the dishes. Finally, though, she couldn't stay inside another minute.

Nobody was in the campground. Even Josh was gone. She knew he hadn't gone with the others, and she suspected he was off talking to his Father.

Josh didn't come back until evening. Maggie hadn't known if he'd be back at all, so she hadn't fixed anything to eat. Anyway, she figured she was probably the last person he'd want to see.

She'd been sitting in a lounge chair for over an hour, thinking about Chance and wishing she could at least talk to someone about him, when she saw Josh coming toward her. Maggie sat bolt upright. She wanted to run away before he got there. She could only imagine how much she'd disappointed him by staying behind. Her spot in the caravan was wasted. What good was she if she just rode along, afraid to do anything?

Josh sat in the chair beside her. His expression was as warm and full of love as ever. Sighing, he leaned back in the chair. "The Lord's unfailing love continues forever."

Maggie recognized it from the book of Psalms.

"I'm here if you want to talk, Maggie." He smiled at her before closing his eyes, as if resting. "You know that, don't you?"

Maggie did know that. And on the one hand, there was nothing she wanted more than to talk about Chance. She'd talked to Josh about almost everything else—everything, that is, except Chance. That was a big "except." But she couldn't quite bring herself to do it. What could she say? That she was sorry? She was. But as much as she wanted to tell him how she felt, she couldn't. She trusted Josh more than any other man she'd ever known. But it wasn't enough.

Josh stayed there with her as the evening wore on and lightning bugs flashed in the dark sky. He hummed songs Maggie had never heard, songs with rich, full melodies that made her think about heaven and a time when she could be the person God the Father wanted her to be. Josh didn't leave her the whole night, and he was still sitting right beside her when she woke up the next morning.

❧

Bob and Brad were the first ones to come running out of the pickup and into camp, where Josh and Maggie were waiting.

"Hey, Sons of Thunder!" Josh called.

The boys both talked at once, reporting how they'd been able to cure a man with cancer. In a Youngstown café, they'd met with a dozen people, who broke down and said they wanted to follow Josh. Maggie had trouble taking it all in because they talked so fast.

"Just a minute, now," Josh said, laughing with them. "Don't forget. It's not that you could do all of these things. That's not what you need to be excited about. Celebrate the fact that these people will be in heaven with us!"

The others returned every bit as jazzed as the Sons of Thunder. They'd been part of miracles. They'd helped people find one another, and find Josh. Maggie was touched by their courage and the way God had used them. But it made her feel worse that she hadn't gone with them.

She wondered if they were all asking themselves the same question she was: Why did Josh put up with Maggie Dale?

Chapter Twenty

After that, Maggie began to keep to herself even more. They were all so busy that she didn't think anyone even noticed. Josh spent more and more time with Pete and Brad. Sometimes they'd go off together, and the others wouldn't see them for the rest of the day. They were staying in rustic cabins in Ohio's Appalachian country, around Hocking Hills, where the Native Americans had settled Ohio.

When Josh disappeared again

with Pete and Brad, Maggie took advantage of the down-time by sleeping in.

She was rushing over to the dining hall to try to get something to eat before it closed for breakfast, when she saw a crowd gathering in the valley. Her first thought was that word had gotten out that Josh was staying here.

"Maggie!" Matt trotted up to her. "You haven't seen Josh, have you?" He sounded worried.

Maggie shook her head. "What's up?"

Before Matt could answer, Miguel ran up. "You better come! Fast!"

They hurried toward the commotion in the valley, where a crowd had formed in a circle, and people were shouting. Thad came over to them and lowered his voice. "I don't know what to do. There's a kid—something's wrong with him. His dad brought him here for Josh, but Josh isn't here."

Maggie shoved her way through the mass of bodies until she saw what the crowd was staring at. A boy, who might have been ten or eleven, lay on the ground. His back was rigid, his jaw clenched. A thin man, obviously his father, squatted beside him, holding him, as the boy shook violently. Maggie knelt beside the boy's father. "What's the matter with him?" She touched the boy's cold forehead.

"He has these fits," the man explained. "I asked those men to help, but it didn't do any good!" He pointed to Thad and Miguel.

Miguel rubbed his stubbled chin. His face contorted. "I tried! I did everything I could think of, Maggie. I don't know what else to do. Matt and Phil tried, too."

Maggie glanced around wildly for help. People were

Dandi Daley MacKall

backing away, as if they were afraid they'd catch whatever was wrong with the boy. Then she saw Andy coming toward them, taking his time. Maggie stood and yelled at him. "Andy! Come here! Quick! You have to help this boy! Hurry!"

Andy glanced at the boy, then back at the father. "Tell me what's wrong with him."

"We've had him to doctors all over the world. They've called it everything from an epileptic fit to meningitis to a neurological abnormality—I don't know!" He tried to hold down his son's shoulders so he wouldn't roll away. "Please help him!" he begged.

Andy put his hands on the boy's head and closed his eyes. After a minute, Andy opened his eyes, but the boy still lay there, thrashing. Andy tried again.

"It's not working, Andy!" Maggie screamed. "Do something!"

"Here! Let me try!" Nate, the lawyer, bent down and pounded on the boy's chest, then breathed into his mouth. There was no change.

Jude grabbed Tom and pulled him over to the boy. "Come on! Let's at least move him to the grass." They hoisted him up—Jude at his head, and Tom at his feet.

When they were almost to a soft patch of grass, the boy jerked his arms and legs. He twisted his whole body. Jude and Tom tried to hold on, but the boy slipped out of their grasp.

Maggie screamed as he hit the ground and rolled over. "Help him!" What good was any of this if they couldn't save this one boy? "Can't any of you do anything?" she pleaded.

"I tried!" Jude shouted back. "It's not *my* fault. Andy's the one who—"

"Me? What about Matt?" They argued about who should try again.

Maggie's panic grew until she couldn't think straight. Leaning over the boy, she reached out to comfort him. But his arms were flailing. Maggie ducked, but not in time. His fist landed on her jaw, the impact knocking her backward.

Shaking it off, she cried out, "Where's Josh? Why isn't he here when we need him?"

"Maggie! Are you all right?"

Jessica dropped to her knees beside Maggie, but Maggie refused to look at her. What did Jessica know about losing a child?

"Is that Josh?" Matt squinted toward the parking lot.

Maggie stood up and shaded her eyes, straining to see. Four men were walking down the hill. Maggie recognized Brad and Josh. "Josh!" she screamed, running as fast as she could toward them. Bob and Pete were there too. "Josh! Where've you been?"

"What's all the arguing about down there?" Pete asked.

"We needed you!" Maggie yelled. "You can't take off like that when people need you! Hurry! There's a little boy! He's dying!"

She grabbed Josh's arm, dragging him with her to where the boy lay writhing on the ground. "Help him!" she demanded.

The crowd, much bigger now, closed in on them. Bob and Brad had to hold some of the people back so Josh could make it through. Matt, Andy, and the others pressed in close

Dandi Daley Mackall

to Josh, making excuses and telling them what they'd tried to do to help.

The boy's father lifted his arms to Josh. "Please! He's my only son! He has these terrible seizures! They've almost killed him. You weren't here, so I asked your people to help him, but they couldn't do anything."

Josh turned to Andy, Nate, Matt, and the others. "What's it going to take for you to believe?"

Suddenly the boy jerked violently. He writhed on the ground, kicking and flailing his arms. White foam oozed from his mouth.

"Josh!" Maggie cried. "Do something!"

Josh, still calm, turned to the child's father. "How long has this been going on?"

"Since the day he was born. It's like something inside him wants him dead, like there's a war inside my boy. Please! Help us! If there's anything you can do, please!"

Josh put his arm on the man's shoulder. "*If? If* there's anything I can do?" he repeated softly. "Everything is possible if you believe."

The boy's father looked panicked. "I do believe! Just . . . just help me not to doubt."

Josh looked to heaven, then prayed over the boy. He commanded the boy to be well and ordered whatever was warring inside of him to get out.

The boy screamed. It was an unearthly noise that Maggie knew would stay with her for the rest of her life. He threw himself backward into another violent convulsion. His eyes rolled back into his head. Maggie thought it would never end. She heard her own screams but couldn't silence them.

Then the boy stopped. He lay there without moving.

Maggie ran to him. "He's dead!" Sobbing, she laid her head on the boy's chest. Why had she ever come here? Why did she have to see this?

Murmurs filtered through the crowd. She heard scoffing, the news traveling fast that the boy was dead, in spite of all that Josh and his followers had tried to do.

Then Josh knelt down beside Maggie and took the boy's limp hand in his. "Come on, son."

The boy's chest moved, and Maggie jumped away. His eyes fluttered open. They were beautiful—big and brown. Then, still holding on to Josh's hand, he got to his feet. Josh guided the boy to his father, who seemed to be frozen. The boy walked up and took his father into his thin arms. They hugged and cried.

"It's okay, Dad," the boy whispered. "I'm fine."

Cheers rose all around them. Everybody wanted to talk to the boy and his father.

Josh and the others managed to slip away to the dining hall. Maggie followed them, as if she were in a dream. She'd seen it happen. It was a miracle. But her hands were still shaking, and she couldn't stop crying, even now.

Andy took the seat next to Josh at the big dining-hall table. "Josh, why couldn't we do anything?"

"You didn't have enough faith," Josh answered.

"We have faith," Jude countered.

Josh shook his head. "If you had faith as tiny as an atom, you could tell the state of Ohio to move to Africa and it would. Nothing would be impossible."

Maggie got up and walked off by herself.

Dandi Daley Mackall

Faith. What did she know about faith? She'd been half crazed watching that boy suffer. Her throat still burned from screaming. She hadn't been able to call up an ounce of faith or trust in Josh. She hadn't even tried.

Chapter Twenty-one

Maggie took to riding in the RV because it was easier to avoid Josh that way. They drove north to Ashtabula, then followed the lake back west, going into Cleveland again. Maggie worked hard, but she kept in the background, preparing meals, getting supplies, cleaning up, staying out of the way. They traveled through Wooster and on over to Mansfield. Everywhere they went, they were met with crowds.

In downtown Mansfield, Josh spoke at a scheduled Community

Hall service, and people loved him. They would have kept him there all day, but Jude had scheduled three other talks that afternoon. As they left the building, the whole congregation followed them, and more people were waiting outside on the steps and sidewalk. Even the street was packed with people trying to get a glimpse of Josh.

"We need to get to the parking lot!" Tom shouted.

Jude was snapping photos. Pete and the Sons of Thunder acted as bodyguards to keep the crowds from crushing Josh. Maggie hung on to Matt and tried to keep up.

Suddenly the whole crowd came to a halt. Maggie peered around Matt and saw that a man in an expensive suit had elbowed his way to Josh. He'd had the help of half a dozen friends.

"It's Dr. Jared," Matt whispered.

Maggie recognized the name. Jared was the leader of the biggest Worship House in Mansfield. Everything Maggie had heard about him was good. He'd helped set up the local children's charities.

Dr. Jared looked out of breath and panicked. "I need you! Please! My little girl's been in an accident! A horrible car crash. They're taking her to the hospital. She's dying. My wife is with her. Please! Please come and save my daughter!"

"Of course," Josh answered, moving with the man, as the man's friends and the Sons of Thunder tried to clear a path to the limo across the street. But the crowds wouldn't leave him alone. They followed, pressing at him from all sides.

Suddenly Josh stopped in the middle of the street.

Maggie wanted him to keep going. She pushed Matt to try to keep the crowd moving forward. All she could think of was the child in the hospital, the little girl dying.

Josh glanced around at the crowd, as if he were searching for someone. "Who touched me?"

People threw up their hands and shook their heads, denying they'd touched him.

"I didn't!" shouted a teenage girl Maggie had definitely seen touch Josh.

"It wasn't me!" said the guy next to her.

"Who cares?" Maggie muttered. "Just go!"

But people kept protesting that *they* hadn't touched Josh and didn't know who had.

Finally Pete pointed out, "Josh, the whole crowd is pushing up against you."

"No kidding!" Brad added.

Josh didn't budge. If Maggie had been close enough, she would have shoved him to the limo. "I'm telling you," Josh said evenly, "someone deliberately touched me. I could feel power coming out of me."

Maggie glanced at the girl's father, Dr. Jared. His face was a portrait in agony.

Then a frail woman stepped from behind Brad and inched toward Josh. She wore a faded green shirt, frayed jeans a couple sizes too big, sandals, and a backward baseball cap. Maggie had no idea how old the woman was, maybe forty or fifty. She shifted her weight from foot to foot, as people grew quiet.

Maggie could see the woman swallow hard.

"Me. I did it," the woman admitted. Her words began

to tumble out, as if they couldn't stay inside her another second. "I touched your shirt. I was infected with HIV, and I've been dying by inches for years. I've tried everything—every new treatment, every drug. My husband left me. I don't see my children anymore. I've been living on the streets because I've spent everything I have on so-called cures."

Maggie could see the color returning to the woman's cheeks. A smile spread across her face.

Then Maggie turned to Dr. Jared. He stood there, twisting his hands and staring silently at Josh. She felt his anguish. They had to go. Josh had to leave *now*. Maggie pushed past Matt and whispered to Pete, "You have to get Josh to the hospital! That little girl—!"

Pete pressed a finger to his lips to shush her and turned back to listen to the woman. Maggie was incensed. Didn't they care about the little girl? Had everybody forgotten about *her*?

Still, the woman kept talking, describing every doctor she'd visited, all the false promises, the treatments, the trips to Mexico. She wouldn't shut up. "You have no idea what I've been through!" On and on she went. "Then I heard you were here." She grasped Josh's hand. "And I touched you. I knew that if I did, you'd cure me!"

Maggie couldn't stand it any longer. "Josh! We have to go!" she urged. "That little girl in the hospital!"

Josh didn't seem to hear her. He smiled down at the woman and squeezed her hand. "Everything's all right now. Your faith has cured you. God's blessed you."

Josh smiled over at Maggie. She knew he was asking her to trust him. But she couldn't. All she could think of was that girl dying in the hospital. And this woman was fine now. Couldn't they just go? Now!

The woman asked Josh something else, and he answered her, but Maggie couldn't hear it. Her head buzzed with anger and frustration. Why didn't they move?

Dr. Jared's attention was focused on something else now. His eyes widened as a man, who looked a bit like him, walked up. "I'm sorry." The man broke into sobs. "Your little girl is dead. I . . . we don't need to bother Josh with it anymore."

Maggie burst into tears. Matt tried to put his arm around her, but she pushed him away. "I told you!" she snapped.

Josh turned to the grieving father. "Don't be afraid. Just trust me, and she'll be all right."

Maggie didn't want to hear the rest. "It's *not* all right!"

Pete shot her a look of utter shock, as if she'd grown another head.

Maggie didn't care. Yes, they'd all be all right in the New World, whenever that came. In eternity.

But what about now? What about a child who would never grow up? never be married? never have children of her own? What about the child lying dead in the hospital? Couldn't they see that this father was torn into pieces? Didn't they understand? Any of them? The man had just lost his daughter because Josh hadn't gotten there in time. What kind of world was it, where children could die?

Josh walked with the man to his limo, and Pete got in with them. The others ran to their cars. Maggie followed Matt to the RV, but she didn't talk to anybody on the drive to the hospital, not even when Matt asked her if she was okay.

The drive seemed to take forever. Krystal and Brad were laughing, as if everything were normal. "I love that woman!" Krystal exclaimed. "You could see her getting better, right before our eyes! And when Dr. Jared and the others see what Josh will do for his daughter, can you imagine? They'll all believe in him!"

Maggie shut them out. She'd heard what the man told Dr. Jared. She'd seen the agony in the doctor's eyes. She'd recognized it, felt it herself.

When Matt shut off the engine in the hospital parking lot, Maggie stayed where she was. She didn't want to go inside, but she couldn't stay outside either. She waited until everybody else emptied out of the RV. Then she followed them, staying back, out of the way. She watched which floor their elevator stopped at, then took the next elevator.

When she got off, it was easy to tell which room was the girl's. A crowd huddled together in the hall. Two women were wailing desperately. Their cries ripped into Maggie's soul. Other children stood around the women, crying and hanging on to their legs.

Maggie walked closer and stood beside Matt. "Where is he?"

Matt nodded at the hospital room. "Josh is inside with the parents. Pete, Bob, and Brad went with him. He didn't want anybody else to go in."

Andy walked up. "What do you think they're doing in there?"

It took all the willpower Maggie had not to break into tears or explode in a blind rage.

Sally appeared outside the room. Maggie hadn't seen her since the Community Hall service ended and everything had gone wrong.

"Stop crying, everyone!" Sally smiled at the sobbing relatives. "Josh said that little girl will be all right. So she's going to be just fine!"

An old woman let out a bitter laugh. "She's dead! My grandbaby's not fine. She's dead!"

Another woman, a generation younger, chimed in. "Why did they let him in there? He's too late."

"Seriously," a doctor muttered, "who does this guy think he is? He's not a doctor. And we're not idiots. The girl's dead."

"Why didn't Josh come sooner?" asked a young man, his arm around one of the older women.

Maggie could have shouted, "Amen!" to that. Josh should have come the minute he heard the girl was dying.

At that instant, the door to the hospital room opened, and Josh walked out. He winked at the nurse standing closest to the door. "I'll bet she's hungry. How about some ice cream?"

The nurse took a step inside the room and gasped. "You're alive!"

Everyone rushed to the door. Heart pounding, Maggie made her way close enough to look inside. A pretty girl in a faded green hospital gown was being smothered in kisses by her mom and her dad, Dr. Jared. The girl was standing beside the bed, laughing.

Relatives rushed into the room. Everyone was yelling and laughing and crying at the same time. Out in the hall, Krystal and Sally hugged each other and spun in circles down the corridor. Doctors ran in from all over the hospital.

Then Josh turned and smiled directly at Maggie. And she knew that he knew. He'd seen how she'd failed to trust him again. He knew that her faith was less than nothing. He understood the agony she'd put herself through by not believing him. And he'd already forgiven her.

How could he keep doing that? Forgiving her over and over?

But it didn't matter. She couldn't forgive herself. And she was no good to anyone else, certainly not to Joshua Davidson.

Maggie turned and ran out of the hospital. She was never coming back.

Never.

Dandi Daley Mackall

Part 3

Chapter Twenty-two

Dear Chance,

I'm sorry I haven't written. I've put
it off so long because I've been too
ashamed to write. Once a coward,
always a coward, huh? But I promised
you the truth, no matter how ugly. So
here goes.

Things haven't been going so
great since I quit Josh and his
followers.

I know that I've been born again.
"Born of the Spirit," Josh called it. I'm
not "unborn" or anything. I still

belong to Josh and the Father. In a weird way, I'm probably
more sure of that than ever because I've done everything I can
to get Josh out of my head. But I can't. He whispers to me
when it's quiet. He shouts when I'm high. He's everywhere I go.

I'm back at the bar. The boss made me beg to get my
old job back, but he's letting me stay in the little room
above the bar. Docking my salary for it, of course.
I don't care. I don't seem to care about much these days.

I miss talking to Josh. I miss that more than
anything.

Maggie stuffed the letter into her pack and walked
over to the sink. She ran the water to get the iron smell out
before filling her glass. Watching the water splash into the
sink made her remember the day Sam had run into the bar
with her story about Josh and the "living water" he'd
promised her.

Maggie shook her head. Even here, even now, Josh
wouldn't leave her alone.

She filled her glass, shut off the water—hard—and
took two Vicodin. She'd bought a dozen of them, along
with some Oxy and weed from one of Matt's old friends.
Her heart was pounding. Tears pressed against her eyes as
she remembered all the other times she'd drugged herself.

Before Josh. Before he'd changed everything.

Yet now . . .

Maggie didn't want to think about it. She didn't want
to remember. She didn't want to feel. That's why she'd
bought these blasted pills.

She hadn't run straight from Josh back to drugs. She'd

Dandi Daley Mackall

stopped off at her mother's first. When the bus had dumped her back in Slayton, she had walked the three miles to the farm and found her mother jarring pickles in the kitchen. Her mom hadn't shown the slightest pleasure or relief in seeing her daughter. She had stopped slicing cucumbers only long enough to shout, "I know where you've been and what you've been doing! I can't even go out of the house without someone telling me about my daughter and those men she runs with. Everybody knows the kind of things you people do with each other!"

Maggie hadn't said a word. She'd turned around and walked all the way back to the bar. . . .

By the time Maggie got downstairs, the pills had deadened her senses. She wasn't using like she had before she met Josh. No coke. But she kept a good supply of pot and painkillers.

When she'd started working again at the bar, she'd struggled to stay clean. The first day she'd poured herself a whiskey, then dumped it out before she could drink it. She'd fought the restlessness, the guilt, the loneliness, for two full days before giving in. She'd thought about calling Sam but was too embarrassed. She had voice mail from Jessica, Krystal, Matt, and Andy, but she erased the messages without listening to them. Maggie hadn't told anyone where she was.

After the first drink, she'd told herself that was it. She wouldn't give in again. But she had. And it had gotten easier.

Only nothing could make her feel how she'd felt when she was with Josh. But being with Josh wasn't an option anymore.

Gary and his buddies were already drinking when Maggie started her shift. She returned their greetings and fell into her routine—setting out glasses, checking the inventory, getting the ice out of the machine, wiping down the bar, filling the shakers. Most of the guys had even stopped giving her a hard time for being away so long. It was almost as if she'd never been gone.

But it wasn't, really. Before, she'd had no idea what it was that she was missing. Now she knew. She'd experienced life with Joshua—real life. And she knew that life was still out there, waiting for her to choose it. She just couldn't do it.

"Hey, Maggie!" Gary shouted. "Your old buddy's on TV!"

Maggie's chest tightened, but she hid her emotions as she walked over to the set. At the bottom of the screen, it read *"Columbus, Ohio. Thousands turn out for the first annual Joshua Parade. Terrorist Threat level elevated to orange."*

"Looks like you left too soon, Maggie honey." Gary took a swig of his beer and wiped his mouth with the back of his hand. "They're throwing that Joshua fella a parade. Right down the center of Columbus. How do you like that?"

Maggie took the stool next to him. "I think it's great." She meant it. It was wonderful to see the whole state finally recognizing how amazing Josh was. She saw him sitting in a yellow convertible with Pete, Brad, and Bob. Behind them was the RV. Maggie couldn't help smiling to herself as she remembered the first day Krystal had brought the thing to the Metropark. The day they'd heard the news about Crazy John. It seemed like decades ago. Another lifetime.

Dandi Daley Mackall

High school bands marched. There were color guards and horses and uniformed soldiers. People lined the streets and cheered, throwing confetti and streamers. It was the exact opposite of what she'd been afraid would happen when they finally got to Columbus. Maggie decided she must have misread that, too, because there they were in Columbus, laughing and enjoying the parade. It was a celebration, and they deserved it.

❖

The next day, when Maggie came down to open the bar, she turned on the TV, hoping they'd replay clips of the parade. She switched to the news, where a reporter was interviewing two men. She started setting up tables as she listened.

"You know that he's not had any formal religious training. His origins are questionable. I wouldn't bother bringing it up, except I think he's really gone too far this time."

"Tell us what exactly happened after the parade in Columbus, when you invited Joshua Davidson to be guest speaker at your Community service."

"Yeah. Well, we thought it would be the right thing to do, to host his visit to our city. We were wrong. He didn't waste a minute on pleasantries. I'll tell you that. Instead he launched into some tirade about how we were leaving God—whom he referred to as his Father, something I personally found offensive and egotistical—out of our Community services. He

accused us of gross compromises in society. He offended
all of us, one way or another, claiming we only came
to service to show off our new clothes or to help our
businesses. He thinks we don't give enough money to
other countries, to starving people—as if he'd know
how much we give! That's our business! We weren't
multiracial enough for him, didn't include enough
economic groups. Our heart wasn't in our work. Things
like that. He went on and on."

"And people didn't react well?"

"I should say not! And who can blame them? Honestly! Some of our people had been right down there on
the street throwing confetti. They stormed out of the
service, walked right out in the middle of Joshua's
talk—if you can call his scathing remarks a talk."

"Excuse me for interrupting, but that's almost
exactly what he did at our Worship House. Mr. Davidson
came to our House after he left your service, I believe.
We'd invited him to worship with us. Instead, he took
over! Uninvited, I might add. He went into a lecture
about how we Worship House leaders do everything for
show. It was humiliating. He read from the Scriptures
and claimed the prophets were talking about him! I agree
with the Community leader's assessment that this Joshua
is a total egomaniac. He's a fanatic of the worst kind. Do
you know that he actually thinks people are out to kill
him? He thinks there's some big conspiracy afoot. The
man is insane. I think he could be dangerous."

"Dangerous? Are you serious?"

"I've never been more serious in my life!"

Dandi Daley Mackall

Maggie turned it up. She couldn't believe these guys. Yesterday the whole city had turned out to celebrate Josh's arrival in Columbus. Things in Columbus couldn't change that fast. The news media had probably rounded up two bitter, jealous religious leaders to make Josh sound crazy. That was good television, right? Everybody couldn't have turned on Josh overnight.

"Turn it off, Maggie."

Maggie jumped up, startled. She hadn't realized anybody had walked in. Ben stood behind her. She should have smelled his aftershave. She smelled it now, looking at him. When they'd first started seeing each other, he'd used aftershave to hide the cigarette smell. She'd loved the smell of him then. It had been like an invisible connection between them.

"You look good, Maggie," he said, giving her his best smile. "I heard you were back."

She knew she should say something. "I'm back."

"I'm glad." He slid onto the stool next to her. "I missed you."

She stared down at the floor. He was wearing new shoes. Expensive. His suit looked expensive too. Ben was obviously doing well. Everything about him said things were good with him now, different.

"Did you hear me?" His voice was soft, pleading. "I said I missed you."

All she had to do was smile, to say she'd missed him too. He would take her in his arms and hold her. It had been so long since she'd been with a man. She could close her eyes and feel the beating of another person's heart next to hers. Ben wouldn't judge her. He'd make love to her and make her forget, at least for a while. . . .

But that wasn't enough. Not anymore. And it wasn't for her. No matter how badly she'd failed Josh, she still belonged to him. *He* loved her. Not like Ben loved her. Joshua cared for her and wanted her to be her best. He'd given her the only happiness she'd ever known. He'd given her eternal life.

"No, Ben."

"What? What did you say?" His voice was harder now.

Maggie looked up at him, into his deep, blue eyes. She couldn't deny that, in spite of everything, in spite of what he'd done to her, what she'd done to herself with him, in another life with him, she still felt something for Ben.

"No," she said.

Something inside her grew stronger. He gave her his sexy grin again, but it didn't weaken her this time. She had the power to say no. She had it because of Josh.

She said it again. "No."

Ben's face contorted. His hand clenched into a fist.

Maggie took a deep breath and held her ground.

Ben banged the bar twice, then stood up fast. "Fine! I can do better than you any day! I *have* done better than you—every day you've been gone." He stormed out, slipping at the door. Catching himself, he flung the door open and stalked out.

Maggie let out her breath. *Thank you,* she said in her mind. *Thank you.* She was shaking, but she wasn't afraid. She was happier than she'd been since she'd left Josh. Feel-

ing her new life fill her again was like coming to the sur-
face of a lake after holding her breath too long. She wanted
to gasp, to breathe in the spirit, the spirit of Josh.

Chapter Twenty-three

The door to the bar opened again, and Maggie flinched. For a second she was afraid Ben had come back. She wheeled around to see two men—neither of them Ben—step into the bar. One was a burly policeman, tall, with gray black hair and a broad, dimpled chin that didn't fit the rest of his face. The older man, well dressed in a suit and tie, looked familiar.

"Maggie?" The man in the suit came closer. "You don't remember me, do you?"

Just as he said it, Maggie

remembered. "Representative Nicholson!" He was the one who had shown up at Andy's shop the night Maggie's car had refused to start, the night she'd first heard what it meant to be born again. Maggie's face heated up. She tugged at her skirt, as if that would make it longer.

Nicholson smiled. "You remember. That night changed my life." He glanced at the policeman. "I'm sorry, Joe. Maggie, this is a friend of mine, Sergeant Joe Meredith."

Maggie shook the sergeant's hand and motioned for them to sit at a table by the window.

"How about over there?" Nicholson nodded at a table away from the window.

The three of them sat down. They were the only people in the bar.

"Have you seen Josh since that day at the garage?" Maggie asked. "Does he know he changed your life?"

Nicholson grinned. "Who do you think sent me here, Maggie?"

"Josh?" Maggie couldn't believe it. "Is he all right?" She had a million questions. "You've seen him? He . . . he sent you? To see *me*?"

Nicholson nodded.

Maggie couldn't believe it. With all Josh had been doing and planning, with the parade going on in Columbus, had he actually had time to think about *her*? In that instant, she missed him so much it hurt. "He's okay, isn't he?"

"Josh is the same as always. I don't know if you've been keeping track of Josh since you left, but there's a lot happening in Columbus." Representative Nicholson turned to the sergeant. "Joe's a believer in Josh, too. Joe, just tell Maggie what you told me."

Maggie waited. The air conditioner clicked on, and cold air shot out of the vent above their table. She shivered.

Joe glanced around the room before he started. "Word's going around the station house in Columbus that the same kind of thing that happened to Crazy John could happen to Josh."

Maggie stopped breathing. She stared from Joe to Nicholson and back again. "What are you saying? They can't arrest Josh! He hasn't done anything! People love Joshua. They threw him a parade and—"

"Things are changing, ma'am," Joe explained. "Yeah, they threw him a parade when they thought he was coming to do miracles for them. But they don't like the way he's been talking to them and criticizing them. When you get right down to it, a lot of people are afraid of him. And the governor's making things worse. He's been stirring up the press. People think Joshua Davidson is a troublemaker, or something a whole lot worse."

"You know Senator Harold, don't you, Maggie?" Nicholson asked.

Maggie nodded. She remembered what Jessica and Krystal had said about him. They claimed he was more powerful than the governor.

"He hates Josh," Nicholson continued. "Senator Harold has been holding secret meetings in the senate for weeks. He's trying to come up with a legal way to get rid of Josh. He says Joshua Davidson is bad for the state of Ohio and for the entire world. Harold's getting a lot of support, too. I do what I can, but he owns the senate. He controls the state."

"What are we going to do? We have to do something!" Maggie exclaimed.

"That's why we're here." Nicholson lowered his voice, and Sergeant Meredith got out of his seat to check the front door and behind the bar. "I saw Josh before the parade," Nicholson said. "We had a good talk. That's when he told me where to find you."

Shame raced through Maggie, leaving her heart pounding and her skin on fire. Of course Josh had known all along where she was, where she'd run to.

Nicholson went on. "I'm being followed. I don't want to put Josh in any more danger than he's already in. Besides, Josh won't listen to me. Someone has to convince him to leave Columbus and keep a low profile for a while." He paused and studied Maggie. "I thought maybe you could get through to him."

"Me?" She'd turned her back on Josh and walked away. Too much time had passed. She wasn't part of his group anymore. "You don't understand. I haven't kept in touch with anybody. I could give you names of dozens of followers who would do a better job. I-I can't imagine Josh would even want me there now."

"Maggie, you're wrong." Nicholson reached across the table and put his hands on hers. "You're forgetting that Josh is the one who told me where I could find you. He also said that if I caught up with you, he wanted me to pass along a story."

Maggie laughed. "A story?" That was so totally Josh. She leaned back in her chair and waited. Memories of Josh's storytelling flashed through her mind. She saw him capti-vating gangs in Cleveland, baseball fans in Toledo, college students at Kent State.

"Admittedly, I'm not the storyteller Josh is," Nicholson confessed.

"Got that right," Sergeant Meredith teased.

Nicholson forged ahead with a story about a man who threw a party for the most important people in Columbus. But when nobody showed up, the man left his mansion and went to the hospitals, the orphanages, the women's shelters, the soup kitchens, to the alleys and bars, and he invited those people instead. Nicholson finished his story dramatically. "The host threw open his doors to the down-and-outers and declared, 'You're the people I want with me. Come on in!'"

Maggie was sobbing. She could almost hear Josh's voice behind this story, full of acceptance and forgiveness. She grabbed a napkin off the table and dabbed at her eyes. Sniffling, she said, "Once Pete asked Josh how many times he was supposed to forgive Andy. Josh told him, 'As many times as there are numbers.'"

Maggie stood up, ran to the bar, grabbed the pack with all of Chance's letters, and came back to the table. "So, who's driving?"

Chapter Twenty-four

Sergeant Meredith drove, taking the back roads to the I-71 turnoff. Maggie sat in the backseat and leaned forward, sensing the urgency that hung in the silence of the squad car. She tried not to think about anything but Josh, and the fact that he wanted her there with him.

But Josh wasn't the only one she'd be seeing again. He wasn't the only one she'd let down. Jessica, Matt, Pete, and the others had stuck it out. They'd moved on without Maggie.

She'd ignored their attempts to contact her. What if they didn't want her now?

Maggie's chest tightened. Her hands shook. Glancing down, she realized she was still in her bar clothes, a thin tank top and a short denim skirt. That sure wasn't going to help get her back into the good graces of the group. Her knee jiggled and refused to stay still. She felt like ropes were twisting around her lungs, shutting off her air.

Her pack was at her feet, inches away. And inside were her pills. If she took just one, to calm herself down, to help her face people, maybe—

No. She was *not* going to do it. How could she even think about it? Josh had done so much to free her from drugs and everything else. She couldn't do this to him again. Or to herself.

"Sergeant!" Maggie fumbled with her seat belt, trying to get it off. "Pull over, Joe. Please?"

Nicholson turned and frowned at her. "Maggie, are you all right?"

"I just need to take care of something."

Sergeant Meredith stopped the car on the side of the road next to a wide-open field. Maggie grabbed her pack and dashed out of the car and across the ditch. She knelt in the weeds and dug out every last pill from her pack. She kept them in small plastic bags, unmarked. Opening each bag, she dumped the pills and stamped them into the mud until they were out of sight.

Then Maggie breathed in the fresh, clean air of the countryside. Wildflowers bloomed all around her, bravely poking up their heads above weeds and brush.

Dandi Daley Mackall

She ran back to the car, laughing. "*Now* I'm ready."

Joe pressed the speed limit all the way to Columbus. When traffic picked up outside the city, he used his siren to get around it.

"Where are we going?" Maggie asked when they entered the city limits. Orange construction barrels forced traffic into one lane, but there wasn't much Joe could do about it. "How do we find Josh?"

"He's downtown," Nicholson answered. "There's a Community Hall service on the west side. He's supposed to be speaking right about now. We're going to drop you off at the intersection, Maggie, so we don't draw attention. Is that okay with you?"

Maggie nodded. She wished they could go with her, but she understood. "Do you know anything about the people at this service? Are they for Josh or against him?"

Joe shrugged as he turned up an alley. "This is supposed to be the most pro-Josh group in Columbus. Josh should be okay. He's got lots of followers there."

"Or lots of fans anyway," Nicholson added. "I think we're all discovering there's a difference."

They eased to a stop behind a warehouse dock. Nicholson rolled down his window and pointed up the street to a white-stone building. "That's it, Maggie. May God the Father be with you."

Maggie hugged both of them before climbing out. Waving, she backed away from the squad car. It was, she thought, as if she'd known these men her whole life, as if they were her own brothers. A sadness swept over her when she turned and walked away. Maggie had the feeling that she might never see them again.

❖

As Maggie made her way to the Community Hall, people streamed steadily out of the building. Afraid she'd already missed the service, she picked up the pace. But when she got closer, it was clear that the service was still going. A crowd overflowed down the steps and onto the sidewalk, with people standing on tiptoes to see inside. Everybody looked so well dressed. Again, Maggie wished she'd changed clothes.

Then she remembered the wildflowers. If God dressed them, she wasn't going to waste another second worrying about her own clothes. She pressed closer, sliding between bodies wedged together on the stone steps. They gave her dirty looks, like she was shoving in line or crashing the party, but she kept going. More people scurried out of the building, giving Maggie the sensation of swimming upstream.

When she was almost to the top of the steps, she stopped. She couldn't make out the words, but she knew that voice. It was Josh's voice—loud, strong, authoritative. She'd missed that voice. It sounded like home.

But judging by the angry faces around her, people didn't much like whatever Josh was telling them.

Maggie stepped aside to get out of the way of a middle-aged couple rushing out of the hall.

The woman was fuming. "Can you believe he's talking

to *us* like this? Does he know how much we've done for him already? He should be thanking us!"

Maggie tried to tune out the complaints and murmurings as she edged inside and stood in the back.

"Some of you are hoping I'll come up with more free food or water-to-champagne tricks, right?" Josh was saying. "But that's not what all of this is about. *I am* the Bread! You have to devour *me*!"

A distinguished, elderly man, who had been standing next to Maggie, bumped her in his rush to get away.

Josh didn't let up. Maggie had never heard him talk so freely. There were no stories now, no hidden meanings. "What about justice and mercy and faith? There's a plot in this very city to kill me. Don't you understand that you can't destroy me? It's this city, even the entire world as you know it, that will be destroyed!"

There was a mass exodus. People knocked into Maggie as they escaped. Her pack fell from her shoulder, and she went down, landing on the floor with shoes shuffling around her, over her. She saw one of Chance's letters slide across the floor, and she scrambled to crawl after it. Someone kicked her arm. A high heel landed on her fingers as they closed around the letter. She cried out, then struggled to her feet.

Hundreds of people poured past her. She hugged her pack as they jostled her from all sides.

Finally, only a few dozen people remained in the giant hall. Maggie glanced around and spotted Brad.

In that exact moment, he seemed to see her, too, and jogged over to her. "Maggie! You're back!"

He hugged her, and Maggie hugged him back, fighting off tears.

Andy came up behind her and threw his arms around her, too. "I knew it! I told Pete you'd come back! Are you okay?" He helped her hoist the pack back up on her shoulder.

Across the room, Nate yelled to her. Then Phil. She looked around the hall. They were all there. Pete, Jude, Miguel. Everyone. They waved and grinned at her. Matt climbed over benches to get to her. When he did, he lifted her off the ground and spun her around.

Maggie wasn't sure she'd ever felt this happy. It was as if she had never run away from them.

No. It was better. Maybe, for the first time, she felt a part of it all.

They turned back to Josh. He was still standing in front, separated from them by rows and rows of nearly empty seats. Josh kept talking to those few who had stayed. His voice echoed in the emptiness of the great hall. "Do you understand that I have to die for you? I'm pouring out my blood for you. There's no sacrifice without blood! Haven't you read the Scriptures? You need to wash yourselves in my blood for forgiveness!"

Matt frowned down at Maggie. "I don't understand anymore, Maggie. What's he saying? How can he expect these people to get it?"

Some of the remaining listeners got up and walked out.

"I'm afraid he's going to drive them all away," Andy whispered.

Maggie thought Andy looked older. Or maybe this was the first time she'd ever seen him so worried.

Josh stared around the Community Hall at the few followers still with him. "Am I offending you? Just wait. What are you going to think when you see me come back from heaven again? What will you think when you see a new heaven and a new earth replace this one?"

The room kept emptying. One by one, people turned and walked away, until only their small group was left.

"Aren't you going to leave too?" Josh asked them quietly.

Maggie smiled back at him. Then she ran up the aisle and into his open arms. She melted into him, soaking up his strength, his love.

Pete shouted at Josh, "Go? Where would we go? You're the only one offering eternal life." He looked around for nods of agreement and got them.

They closed in around Josh then. Maggie watched them, proud to be part of this group. Josh's gaze met each one of them. And then his face broke into a grin.

Yet before it did, Maggie was pretty sure she'd seen something else on Josh's face. In the flick of an instant, before he'd moved on, Josh had glanced directly at Jude. And he hadn't been smiling.

❖

They were leaving the Community Hall when an older man in a black suit walked up to Josh. "Joshua Davidson?" Behind him were two younger men.

Josh seemed to recognize them. "It's good to see you again," he said, shaking their hands.

The older man frowned. "Linda asked us to come here

and see you personally, instead of just calling and asking for your help. It's her brother, Lawrence. He's very ill. We know what good friends you are with the family. His sisters are afraid for him, and he won't call the doctor or go to the hospital. They want you to come."

Josh smiled back at him. "Lawrence is going to be all right. You tell them that."

The men nodded, then left.

Maggie didn't take her eyes off Josh. It was obvious that he had no intention of following the men. He wasn't going to run to Linda's home and take care of this instantly. She didn't know why. She felt the urge to go with the men herself, but she'd learned the hard way that doubting Josh never got her anywhere. He always knew what he was doing, even if she didn't. This time she knew she could trust Josh. If he didn't run to help Lawrence now, then he had a better plan, something that would do more for the New World, for Linda and Beth, and for Lawrence.

❧

They stayed in Columbus for a few days, and every minute was busy. Jude had booked meetings with politicians. Tom had scheduled services at Worship Houses and Community Halls across the city. But Josh still made time for the woman sitting alone in a coffee shop, the hyped-up teenager on the city bus, the man waiting patiently in the barbershop for a haircut. Josh talked to gangs in dark alleys, to businesswomen rushing to work, to elderly couples sitting on their front porches. But what Maggie liked best was to watch Josh with the children, who found him wherever they went.

A week had passed since they'd received word that Lawrence was sick. Maggie, Josh, and the others were sitting in the back of Antonio's, a restaurant where Josh had taken them a couple of times. They were halfway through dinner when Antonio, the owner, asked to talk to Josh.

Josh scooted over a chair and invited Antonio to sit with them.

Antonio glanced nervously at the door, then took a seat. "Joshua," he began, "there's word throughout the city that someone has put out a contract on you. Someone has paid to have you killed."

Bob exploded. "A contract? What is this? *The Godfather*?"

The restaurant owner shook his head. "This is not organized crime. It's much higher up. I would not tell you this, except on very good authority."

Maggie's heart was pounding so hard her chest heaved. Everything Josh had said came rushing back to her. He'd warned them about the things that were going to happen to him. Representative Nicholson and Joe had trusted her to convince Josh to leave the city, but she hadn't even tried. She'd gotten caught up in Josh's work. He seemed so in control of everything that she hadn't been afraid for him. "Josh, we should leave Columbus, just for a little while."

"Maggie's right," Andy agreed.

Pete jumped to his feet so fast that his chair tipped over. He threw his napkin onto his plate. "I want to know who's behind this! Who wants Josh dead? It's Senator Harold, isn't it?"

Poor Antonio seemed to shrink.

Josh motioned for Pete to sit down again. "I've told all of you from the beginning that this was going to happen. Go on, Antonio."

Maggie realized that she was clutching Matt's hand under the table.

Antonio wiped his sweaty forehead with a cloth napkin. Maggie felt sorry for him. He'd been a good friend to them. "We heard this afternoon that they know about this house of your friends in Harrisburg, where the two sisters and brother live. We buy flowers from the young sister, Beth. My advice is that you stay away from there."

Josh stood up and hugged Antonio. "Thank you, my friend. Don't worry about this. Nothing will happen to me until it's the right time. My Father picks the time and the place." Maggie saw that twinkle in Josh's eye. "And right now, it's time for us to go see our friends in Harrisburg. My old friend Lawrence is sleeping, and I need to go wake him up."

"You know," Matt observed, "if Lawrence is just sleeping, he could probably wake up on his own, right?"

"Lawrence is dead," Josh said plainly.

Tears sprang to Maggie's eyes. She'd barely known Lawrence, but she'd loved him.

"For your sakes," Josh continued, "it's good that Lawrence died. Now you have another chance to trust me."

Maggie was almost certain his words were aimed at her. A silence settled over the table. Maggie was the first one to speak. "When do we leave?" she asked calmly.

Dandi Daley Mackall

Matt stared at her as if he didn't know her.

Then Tom surprised them by standing up so fast that his laptop fell to the floor. "Maggie's right. We're with you, Josh, no matter what! If they want you, they'll have to go through us!"

And one by one, they all agreed.

Chapter Twenty-five

Matt and Andy tried to convince
Maggie to ride in the RV with them.
But Josh was driving the truck, and
Maggie wanted to stay as close to
him as she could. When they reached
Harrisburg, they had to drive a half
mile past Linda's house just to find a
parking place. As they walked back
to the house along the car-lined
road, they passed the Harrisburg
Cemetery. Maggie caught herself
checking out hiding places for assas-
sins, squinting into the fields to see

behind gravestones and trees. She couldn't shake her anxiety. Were they walking into a trap?

Pete and Matt must have felt the same way. They flanked Josh and kept peering around, vigilant as bodyguards. The only one who didn't look worried was Josh.

People dressed in black covered the lawn, moving like ants on an anthill. Two men walked stiffly toward them, and Maggie recognized them as the messengers Linda had sent to Josh in Columbus. When they were close enough, the younger man shouted, "He died! Lawrence is dead. We buried him yesterday."

Jude strode up to them and offered his hand. "We're very sorry for your loss."

Both men turned away and walked back to the house.

Maggie tried to stay close to Josh, as they took the sidewalk to Linda's house. She didn't understand why Josh had waited so long to come, but she trusted him. Josh had loved Lawrence even more than she had.

Linda, her face tear streaked, met them at the door. "Joshua, if you'd been here, my brother wouldn't have died."

"Linda," Josh replied softly, "your brother is going to rise again."

Linda gave him a weak smile. "I know. We'll rise again on Resurrection Day."

Maggie wanted to believe that for Chance. She *did* believe it. But she understood Linda's pain. Linda wanted her brother now.

Josh didn't look away from Linda. "I am the Resurrection and the Life. Those who believe in me will die like

everyone else, but they'll live again. They'll have eternal life for believing in me. Do you believe me, Linda?"

Maggie could read Linda's struggle on her face. "I've always believed you," Linda answered. "You're God's Son."

Beth came rushing past her sister and out to meet Josh. Her beautiful hair was matted, as if she hadn't even bothered to brush it. She flung her arms around Josh. "Why didn't you come? If you'd been here, my brother would still be alive!" Her whole body shook. Tears streamed down her face.

Josh held her, and Maggie saw tears in his eyes, too. Josh was crying with Beth . . . *for* Beth.

Maggie couldn't explain why, but seeing Josh cry with Beth touched her more deeply than anything else. She thought of how she'd cried after the abortion, how she'd thought for days and weeks that she might never stop crying. And the worst part of it all had been that she was crying alone, with nobody to hold on to. Now, as she watched Josh comfort Beth, Maggie believed that she would never have to go through anything alone again. Josh would be there to cry with her.

"Take me to him," Josh said.

The crowd followed Beth and Josh up the road to the cemetery. Billowing clouds raced above them, as if wanting to get there first. Maggie walked with Linda and Matt. But when they got to the freshly dug plot, she stopped to let Linda go ahead.

Josh glanced at Linda. "We need a shovel."

Linda gasped.

"Haven't I promised you that you could see God's glory

if you'd just believe?" Josh's voice was as gentle as the breeze that ruffled Linda's skirt and blew her hair across her face.

Linda stepped back and let it happen. Andy did the digging, while Josh prayed out loud to his Father. It took eight men to lift the casket out of the ground, a carved mahogany coffin with brass railings. Maggie expected Josh to open the lid, like he had for Mrs. Tessler's little boy, Daniel.

Instead he took a step back from the grave and shouted, "Lawrence! Come out!"

Almost immediately the coffin flung open, and Lawrence sat straight up. He looked just like Maggie remembered him, maybe better. She laughed out loud and caught Matt in a bear hug. Then she hugged everybody within reach.

❈

They celebrated at Linda's that night. Linda didn't even have to cook. Neighbors brought in casseroles. Krystal showed up with pastries, pies, and cakes. Maggie wanted the night to last and last. She didn't want to have to think about anything else but being right here with these people, with Josh.

The story of Lawrence's resurrection had leaked to the press within the hour, and everyone wanted a firsthand account. Jude spent most of the night on his cell. Linda had to leave her phone off the hook so she could eat. Maggie hoped that all the attention would make it safer for Josh and scare off any hired killers.

Dinner had been over for a long time, and Pete was in the middle of relating his perfect game for the Toledo Mud Hens, when Maggie noticed Beth coming up behind Josh.

She was holding out her skirt like a blanket and leaving a trail of flower petals as she walked. Eventually the dining room grew quiet. Still Josh didn't turn around. One by one, Beth placed orchids, roses, and exotic flowers on Josh's lap, on his shoulders, at the floor around his feet. She plucked the petals, and let them rain down on him. A sweet fragrance filled the house.

Josh closed his eyes and let it happen.

When Beth was out of flowers, after every petal had been offered to Josh, Jude broke the silence. "Those flowers were worth a fortune! She should have sold them and given us the money. We could have given it to the poor."

Josh's eyes snapped open, and he stared directly at Jude. "Leave her alone. Beth did this to get *me* ready for my death."

The words stung. *Josh's death?* Maggie couldn't imagine her world without Josh.

❀

They drove back to Columbus that night. Josh had been right, of course. Nobody tried to stop them, and he was perfectly safe. His time hadn't come yet. That's how Josh put it.

Maggie rode in the RV to be with Krystal, and they talked the whole way back to the city.

"I love my husband," Krystal confided, "and he does believe in Josh. But he's afraid to speak out. I think I embarrass him."

Maggie did most of the listening, but she found herself caring about both Krystal and her husband. She wouldn't have believed it was possible to love the person she'd most hated in high school, but she did. Josh had changed both of them.

They set up tents in a roadside park just outside the city. Maggie had no idea how much of the night was left, but Josh wanted them to try to catch a couple hours of sleep. "This is it," he said. "Tomorrow we're going back to Columbus. I want you to know what's going to happen."

Maggie tried to read the faces of these people she'd learned to love. They looked as confused as she was.

"When we get there," Josh continued, his face lost in shadows, "I'm going to be betrayed, turned over to the political and religious leaders there, and sentenced to death. They'll spit on me and beat me and mock everything about me. Then they'll kill me."

Maggie had trouble breathing. He'd never spoken this clearly to them. She didn't want it to be true. To be real. To be now.

Josh looked from one to the other. "But after three days, I'm going to rise again."

Maggie wanted to ask a million questions. Did he mean he'd rise to heaven like Elijah? Or did he mean he'd rise for them on earth like Lawrence had risen? She wanted to understand—but she wasn't sure she wanted to know.

Josh walked off into the woods. The rest of them scattered quietly to the tents and the RV. Maggie needed to stay outside under the stars. She headed for the back of the pickup.

Matt and Krystal jogged to catch up with her. "Maggie,"

Krystal whispered, "what does Josh mean? What's he talking about? What's going to happen tomorrow?"

Maggie didn't answer right away. She didn't understand either. But this time she believed. Again she thought of the day she'd watched wildflowers race by outside the truck window, while Josh talked about the Father's care for birds and flowers . . . and for them. And she was ready.

"Tomorrow," she said, echoing Josh's words. "Tomorrow will take care of itself."

Chapter Twenty-six

"You tell everybody what to do, but you don't do it yourselves! You love all the attention you get. You remind me of a cemetery. Your graves are decorated and flowery, but inside, there's nothing but death."

Josh was speaking to the largest crowd ever gathered in Columbus's Capitol Square. Maggie couldn't even guess how many people had shown up. In only 24 hours, word about Lawrence coming back to life had spread all over the world. Some commentators referred to it as a "live burial." Others called it a miracle. Jude had jumped right on it and lined up Josh's biggest appearance yet.

From her seat on the steps of the statehouse, Maggie scanned the crowd for friendly faces. Police roamed the parameters of the square, and security guards were everywhere. She spotted Jessica standing with Josh's mother. Maggie wondered how much Mary Davidson knew about the things that were taking place all over the state. Cleveland had held an anti-Josh demonstration that nearly shut down the entire city. In Cincinnati, political and religious leaders were offering free counseling to "victims of Josh's brainwashing."

Sally moved through the crowd, passing out bottles of water to the elderly. Maggie thought she saw Joe, the police sergeant who had driven her to Columbus.

Josh was getting more boos than cheers. It was hard to believe that these were the same people who had thrown confetti and welcomed him in the parade. "I'm warning you! Get ready for worse wars than you can imagine. The sun will turn black, and the moon won't shine. Stars are going to fall from the sky. Everything you know, everything you see, will be shaken. Heaven and earth are going to pass away, but my words won't."

As Josh read prophetic warnings to them from the Scriptures, people grew more agitated. They didn't like references to the Middle East, even ancient ones.

Maggie wished Josh would go back to telling stories, the way he used to.

"Believe it or not," Josh continued, his eyes brimming with tears, "I've cried over this city. I would have gathered all of you up onto my lap and held you if I could."

The crowd got noisier as the day wore on. Maggie suspected that some of the hecklers had been hired. Fights broke out. Police in riot gear showed up. Still Josh pleaded with people to turn to God and get ready for what was about to happen.

By the time Josh finished, the sun was setting. Police dispersed the crowd, emptying the last stragglers from Capitol Square by force. Maggie and Andy helped pick up trash that had been thrown at Josh.

"Where are they?" Jude paced the Capitol steps.

"Who?" Andy asked.

"The Ohio delegation! They were supposed to be here to welcome us and give us a tour of the statehouse." He glanced at his watch. "They should have been here by now."

"I can live without a Capitol tour," Andy muttered.

Maggie agreed. Her feet hurt.

"I'm going to go find somebody." Jude stormed into the statehouse and fifteen minutes later returned with a guy who appeared younger than Maggie. He reminded her of an elf—he was short, with pointy features.

Jude proudly presented him. "Joshua, everybody, I want you to meet Representative Stephen Fields. Mr. Fields, this is Joshua Davidson."

Josh shook the man's hand.

Fields forced a laugh. "Well, that was entertaining, to say the least. I-I'm sorry none of my colleagues could stick around for the grand finale." He fidgeted with his coat sleeve and glanced out at the square. Streetlights flickered. A night chill had blown in, threatening another storm.

Jude looked so eager to please that Maggie wanted to tell him to stop worrying. "Well, we're all grateful you could be with us, Mr. Fields," Jude said. "We know how valuable your time is. Maybe we can meet some of the other representatives next time." Jude turned to Josh and raised his eyebrows, as if giving some secret signal. "The statehouse here is phenomenal, isn't it, Josh? When was it built?"

Fields sighed. "Ohio used prison labor to start the project in 1839. It took 22 years to complete. It's masonry throughout, with brick and limestone. The foundation is over 18 feet deep, set in pure stone." He paused and eyed Josh. "It would take a lot to bring this building down." Maggie wondered if maybe the representative had been listening after all.

Tom walked up behind her and whispered, "This guy's a pawn of Senator Harold." He patted his laptop. "Research."

Maggie wondered if Jude knew. Or cared.

Jude kept going on and on about the building. "The architecture reminds me of the Parthenon in Greece."

Fields smiled for the first time. "You know architecture?"

Jude shrugged, then Fields continued. "The statehouse was designed after the Greek Parthenon, as part of the Greek Revival. The builders wanted to keep the style as far from English architecture as possible."

Maggie hadn't paid that much attention to the building. Now she took in the center rotunda and the cupola. She tried to remember the name for the plain columns out front, but junior high history was too far behind her. Josh was the one who could have told all of them about the construction of the building. He'd worked construction and carpentry most of his life.

"Would you like me to take you on a tour of the statehouse?" Fields offered.

"That's very generous of you." Jude nodded graciously toward Fields, but his smile faded when he glanced back at Josh. "Don't you agree, Josh? We'd love that, wouldn't we?"

When he swung back to Fields again, Jude's smile was in place. "I've heard this building is as magnificent inside as it is out."

Josh barely glanced at the domed cupola. "These magnificent buildings will be so completely demolished that there won't be one stone left standing."

Fields frowned at Josh. His mouth opened, as if he were going to say something. Then it snapped shut, and he turned and strode back inside the statehouse.

When he was gone, Jude cornered Josh. "Why would you say that?"

"Jude, you could blow down the whole statehouse," Josh answered, "and I could raise it up again in three days."

Maggie glanced around to make sure Fields wasn't still lurking in the shadows. The last thing they needed was for Fields to run back to Senator Harold, or to anybody, and report that Josh had been discussing blowing up the whole statehouse and rebuilding it in three days.

Chapter Twenty-seven

Josh asked Pete to round up everybody and bring them to the statehouse parking lot. City lights clicked on and off, confused by the black sky and flash lightning.

"I have a little surprise planned for tonight," Josh said. "Antonio is letting us use the back room after hours. I know it's late, but I wanted some time alone with you. One last dinner, just us."

As much as Maggie loved the words *just us*, she hated the sound of *one last* anything with Josh.

The drive to Antonio's was quieter than usual. When they got to the restaurant, they piled out of the RV and truck and went straight to the private room Antonio reserved for VIPs. The restaurant was closed on Thursdays, so Nate and Krystal had been appointed chefs and had arrived early to prepare a dinner. Candles burned in the center of a long table. Shadows flickered on the ceiling.

"Everybody, just take a seat," Josh instructed. Maggie sat between Matt and Krystal. Josh disappeared into the kitchen for a few minutes, then returned with salad and bread, which he placed on the table.

"Josh," Krystal said, starting to get up, "let me do that." Josh shook his head, and she sat back down.

"Where's Jude?" Andy asked.

Maggie hadn't noticed he was missing. Everybody else was there.

Nobody answered the question, and it hung in the room with them like cigarette smoke. Maggie wondered if Jude might have gone to the ATM. He handled most of the bill paying and never stopped complaining about their lack of funds.

When Josh took off for the kitchen again, nobody said anything until he got back. This time he had packets of Wet-Wipes. Instead of passing them around, Josh broke open the first packet and unfolded the paper wipe. He started with Matt. "Hold out your hands." When Matt did, Josh washed Matt's hands with the moist towelette. Then he moved around the table, cleansing each person's hands.

When he got to Maggie, she shivered as the tiny cloth touched her palms. She remembered being cleansed the day

Dandi Daley Mackall

she'd let the rain shower down on her, after Josh had brought little Daniel back to life. She'd imagined all the dirt and filth of her life washing back to the gutter. She felt that way again now, and she couldn't stop the tears that came. She wanted to talk to Josh about Chance, to tell him she'd named her baby and never stopped thinking about him.

Josh moved on until he came to Pete.

"No way!" Pete protested. "I can't let you wait on me, Josh!"

Josh opened the packet and took out the tiny cloth. "I'm giving you an example, Pete. Serve other people, just like I'm doing. Besides, if I don't wash you, you don't belong to me."

Pete stuck out both hands. "Then do it! Wash my head too!"

Maggie had to laugh. She loved the way Pete threw himself into things all the way. She envied that.

Josh grinned. "That's okay, Pete. Hands will do." He stopped smiling and glanced around the room. "You're all clean already, except for the one who's decided to betray me."

"Betray you?" Matt asked. "Who's going to betray you?"

"One of us," Josh answered simply.

It was inconceivable for Maggie to think that one of them would ever betray Josh. She wondered what he really meant by it.

The door flung open, and Jude came rushing in. "Sorry I'm late." He took the only empty seat and quickly downed his glass of water. "Did I miss anything?"

They sat there and listened to Jude's account of his

conversation with Fields after the rest of them had left Capitol Square. Jude had lined up a meeting with leading senators, although he hadn't gotten a firm date out of them. As Jude talked, Josh kept making trips to and from the kitchen.

Finally, Josh sat down next to Brad. "I've been looking forward to this dinner for a long time. I wanted to be alone with you before it all starts." He took the loaf of bread he'd brought out and broke off pieces, handing one to each of them. Maggie thought about that day in Cleveland, when he'd fed thousands by doing this same thing with a peanut-butter sandwich. "Eat. This is my body."

He poured the bloodred wine into clear glasses. "It's my blood that seals the promise between you and God. I'm pouring out my blood for the sins of the world."

Maggie thought about what Josh had said in the Community Hall. That they'd have to eat his flesh and drink his blood. It had sounded kind of ghoulish then and made her queasy. It didn't sound that way to her now, though. So many of his followers had run out on him that day. But she'd stayed. She still didn't understand, but she trusted Josh.

After that, they ate the rest of the dinner, and conversation began to flow around the table.

Jude leaned across the table toward Josh. "I was trying to remember what you said out there today. You know, the part about the statehouse coming down. What was that again?"

Josh's expression didn't change. "The statehouse could be destroyed, demolished so that not even one stone remained on top of another, and in three days I could raise it myself."

Jude seemed satisfied with the answer. Maggie decided she'd never figure out the paparazzi. Jude hadn't liked anything Josh had said in front of the politicians today. And now he wanted to hear it again?

As the night wore on, Josh grew more solemn. "I want you to know that the time is now. I'm going back to my Father's home to get a place ready for you. Then I'll come and get you, and you'll always be with me there."

"Take me now, Josh," Maggie pleaded. She knew she should be quiet and just listen to him, but she couldn't. "Take all of us with you. Please?"

"Maggie," Josh replied, "don't you know by now that I'm not going to leave you alone? My Father will send you a guide, the Holy Spirit, who won't ever leave you."

Maggie needed to hear that promise. Josh was talking plainly now. He really was leaving. She didn't want to be afraid, to be a coward and let Josh down. Not this time.

"I'm giving you my peace," Josh said, as if he'd been reading her mind. "My peace isn't like the world's peace. *My* peace is beyond understanding. I'm going away, but I'm coming back again."

"I have no idea where you're going, Josh!" Tom's voice broke. "Just tell us, so we can find you."

"I'm the way, the truth, and the life. Nobody will find the way to the Father without me."

"Wait! We don't need to *find* you," Pete said. "We're coming with you!"

"You can't, Pete. Not now. All of you are going to desert me. But after I'm raised from the dead, I'll meet you and—"

Pete shoved his plate away. The glass in front of him broke. Maggie watched wine soak into the tablecloth. "Desert you? I'm ready to die for you!"

"Die for me?" Josh sighed. "No. Before the sun comes up, Pete, you're going to deny that you even knew me."

All of a sudden, an explosion went off. *Boom! Boom! Boom!* The building shook. Maggie covered her ears. It sounded as if the whole world had imploded.

Dandi Daley Mackall

Chapter Twenty-eight

Maggie screamed. The table rocked. Glasses smashed to the floor. The ceiling rained chunks of plaster onto them. She covered her head.

Then the booming stopped and was replaced by a low rumble. The dining room stopped shaking. The table settled. Maggie looked to Josh. He hadn't moved.

Maggie's heart slowed down. She coughed from the dust still floating around the room.

"Maggie, are you all right?" Brad asked.

Maggie nodded. "Jessica?" She looked around for her friend.

Jessica brushed flakes of ceiling plaster from her hair. "I'm all right. What *was* that?"

Jude sprang up from the table. "I've got to find out what's going on!"

Josh motioned for all of them to stay where they were, but Jude scrambled toward the door anyway. Maggie watched as he climbed over chairs and tables to get to the front of the restaurant. He jerked open the front door and yelled back to them, "It's the statehouse! Somebody's blown up Capitol Square!" Then he ran out.

Nobody else moved.

Gradually Maggie could feel the peace that settled over them. Was this the kind of peace Josh had promised them? Peace beyond understanding? Because she didn't understand.

"We don't have much time," Josh said. "They're going to blame me for this and try to—"

"You?" Pete cried. "Who's going to blame you? That doesn't make any sense!"

Panic was creeping into Maggie's brain, and she couldn't stop it. "Josh, nobody who knows you would believe you blew up anything! They'll know it's terrorism. It has to be!"

Josh nodded. "Of course, they'll know it's terrorism. But they'll use it against me anyway. Don't you understand yet? There's so much I want to tell you, but you can't take it in now. The Spirit will teach you later. When you don't see me anymore, just remember that you will see me again."

Matt whispered to Maggie, "What does he mean we won't see him?"

Others were whispering around the table too. Maggie didn't think any of them had answers. Outside, police sirens blared. Horns honked nonstop. A voice was shouting over a loudspeaker somewhere, but the words sounded like thunder.

"I know you don't understand. I know you'll be mourning everything that's about to happen to me. But I'll see you again."

Without changing his expression, Josh simply started talking to his Father: "Father, this is it. The only thing I want is for people to see you and give you credit for everything you are and all you do. I want you to be glorified. And I pray for my friends here. Take care of them. Take care of the people who will believe because of them."

Maggie couldn't stop crying. Josh was leaving. The horrible things he'd said would happen to him were about to happen. And yet here he was . . . praying for *them*.

Josh led the way to the parking lot, where they all piled into the RV together. Maggie knew where Josh would be heading—to the park. One last time.

It wasn't an easy drive. In the few blocks to their destination, they must have passed a hundred speeding police cars, all heading toward Capitol Square. Maggie moved toward the front of the RV to be closer to Josh. He rolled down the driver's window. She could smell burning tar and smoke. They turned into the park and drove up the lane. Apple trees in bloom lined both sides of the road, and their sweet scent mingled with the stench of death, making it all seem unreal.

"I'm the root and the trunk of the apple tree," Josh said. Maggie moved around so she could see his face in the rearview mirror. She wanted to see that twinkle in his eyes, the one he got whenever he started a story like this. "My Father is the gardener, the orchard keeper. And you—you're the limbs of the tree. Now, the gardener has to cut off every branch that doesn't produce fruit, right? You've already been pruned so you'll be more fruitful. Just stay in me. A branch cut off from the trunk can't grow apples, no matter how hard it tries. You have to be connected to the tree."

They were all quiet. Josh parked the RV and turned off the ignition. For a second he just sat there, his hands on the steering wheel, his head resting on his hands. "I've loved you like my Father has loved me." He turned and faced them. "Now love each other that way."

They walked into the park together. Then Josh took Pete, Bob, and Brad farther in with him. Maggie sat at a picnic table with Jessica. They prayed together. Maggie remembered the time they'd sat at a picnic table together in the Cleveland Metropark, when Maggie's soul had been stung with guilt for having ended Chance's life. That sting was still there. But so much more was there with it now— forgiveness, understanding, love.

They prayed for a long time. Maggie didn't know how many hours had passed when she looked up and saw Josh coming over the hill alone. "Jessica, here he comes," she whispered.

Maggie heard sirens in the distance. Their high-pitched blares grew louder and louder. They were getting closer. From all sides of the park, police sirens screamed. Brakes squealed.

They were pinned down. Caged. Trapped.

"They're coming this way!" Matt shouted, racing past Maggie. "Run, Maggie!"

She stood but remained where she was. Beams of red light swirled through the leaves and grass. Someone was shouting over a police horn, "Give it up! You're under arrest!"

It was inconceivable that they'd come to arrest Josh. If they'd known him at all, they would have known he wasn't guilty of anything.

Maggie heard Jessica scream. Footsteps pounded the dirt all around her. She saw Bob and Pete run off into the woods. Tom fell and scrambled up again, clutching his computer and dragging one leg. She looked around wildly.

Josh still stood at the top of the hill. Watching. Waiting.

Doors slammed. Maggie heard the crack of rifles being cocked.

"We've got you covered!" came the voice over the police horn. "You're surrounded. Come out with your hands up!"

Still Josh stood. Alone.

"Stop it!" she screamed. "He didn't do anything!"

A policeman ran past Maggie, bumping her shoulder and knocking her to the ground. She stayed there. Soldiers or national guardsmen raced past her. They carried shields and guns, as if they were facing down an enemy army.

Another group of armed men raced toward Maggie. They ran over her, as if she weren't there. Someone's boot crushed her ankle. She cried out, unable to move.

They swarmed the hill, closing in on Josh. They were hungry monsters, let out of their den in search of prey.

Maggie squinted back toward the lane. The apple trees were still there, dark and ominous now. She could see the RV, still parked under the branches. Police were already crawling all over it. Under it. A police van was parked in front of it. The door of the police van opened. The inside light flicked on.

Maggie saw Jude sitting in the front seat.

She turned back to Josh, just as the wave of soldiers, police, and national guardsmen reached him. He hadn't moved. He hadn't run. He hadn't tried to escape.

Four armed officers jumped on him, knocking him to the ground. Maggie screamed. She saw their arms move up, then crash down on Josh. Over and over. She heard the flesh give and saw the blood flow.

They cuffed his hands behind his back and dragged him down the hill. Dragged him like a downed kite. Like a sack of garbage.

Maggie tried to stand up, but her ankle gave way, and she fell again. She could see Josh's face. Blood dripped from his nose and mouth, trickling down his shirt.

The earth tilted. It rocked.

Trees spun.

The black sky closed in on her.

Then she couldn't see. There was nothing but blackness. There was nothing at all.

  Dandi Daley Mackall

Chapter Twenty-nine

Dear Chance,

I have fourteen hours and nine minutes to stop this. How many hours, how many days and weeks have I wasted crying, telling myself this can't be happening? This is the twenty-first century! This is the Midwest! This is Ohio! How could such an injustice go on here? Now? How could the whole world be killing the only innocent man who ever lived?

But it is happening. And if

I can't do anything to stop it, the only innocent human being ever to walk the earth will die at midnight.

❖

So much had happened since the night they'd arrested Joshua Davidson. Shell-shocked, Maggie had limped through the city of Columbus for the rest of the night. The entire downtown area had become a war zone of rubble and fire. She'd wandered up and down streets, hoping to run into Pete or Brad or one of the others.

She had been passing a department-store window when she saw Pete's face. Maggie stopped and stared at the television sets displayed in the window. There was Pete, wide-eyed and angry, his face dirty and his shirt torn at the collar. Behind him, firemen worked to put out a fire in Capitol Square, while police struggled to keep the crowd behind a barricade of yellow tape.

Maggie had hobbled inside the store to hear what Pete was saying. The newsman was firing a question at him: "You were with Joshua Davidson, weren't you?"

Pete shoved the mike out of his face and swore. "I told you before! I never knew him! Leave me alone!"

During Josh's trial, Krystal had taken them into her home in Columbus. They'd lived together there.

Josh's mother came and went the whole time. Maggie didn't know how Mrs. Davidson survived the agony of watching her son—so kind, so good—be hated and condemned by the whole world.

They'd watched the arraignment together on television, as live TV sent images of a battered Joshua all over the world. His bruised and bloody face had been barely recognizable. Outside the courthouse, riots took place every day, with angry mobs shouting, "Kill the terrorist! Death to traitors! Death to Josh!"

Nobody was looking for the real terrorists. They had Josh, and that was all that mattered.

The senate held its own investigation, headed by Senator Harold. Harold had been ruthless, leaking false reports about Josh to the media daily. In a unique alliance, he and the governor of Ohio had presented their findings in a joint news conference, standing side by side, as if they were old friends, instead of lifelong enemies.

The trial had been televised by CNN, FOX News, and all the major networks. People all over the world had watched and cheered for the prosecution, as witness after witness got on the stand and told lies about Josh. A woman from Youngstown claimed that she'd heard Josh tell her family that he wasn't a citizen of any country, that his allegiance belonged "somewhere else." Worship House and Community Hall leaders paraded onto the witness stand to explain to the jury the damage Josh's lies had created.

People testified that Josh had threatened the city with war and famine. They said he was obsessed with bloodshed and destruction, all in the name of making room for some fantastic "New Earth." The press picked up the theme, and Josh was portrayed as a fanatic, a religious terrorist of the worst kind.

It had been horrible to watch Joshua Davidson on

trial, but Maggie and the other women had watched it all. They'd gone to the courthouse every day and sat in the gallery, while people lied about Josh. Maggie had been in the courtroom the day the prosecution called its star witness, Jude Smith, to the stand.

Jude produced tapes he had gathered as a government informant. He'd worn a wire the night of their last dinner together. The jury listened, their faces taut and dark, as the tape played:

> "The statehouse could be destroyed, demolished so that not even one stone remained on top of another, and in three days I could raise it myself."

The people had gone wild. They screamed and shouted and tried to get at Josh. The judge had to clear the courtroom. After that, Maggie and the other women weren't allowed in. They'd had to watch the proceedings on television.

Since Josh refused legal counsel, he'd been appointed as his own defense attorney by the state. He sat quietly throughout the prosecution's entire case, through the mockery of a trial. And when it was his time to defend himself, he didn't.

"Don't you understand the charges against you?" the judge demanded. "I can sentence you to death."

"You'd have no power at all if my Father didn't give it to you," Josh answered.

The jury deliberated one hour before finding Joshua Davidson guilty on all counts of murder and terrorism.

 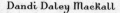 Dandi Daley MacKall

When the sentence was pronounced—death by lethal injection—the crowds around the courthouse cheered. And the cheers reverberated around the world.

Chapter Thirty

"Joe's here, Maggie. Waiting for you downstairs."

Jessica stuck her head into the room where they'd been sleeping on and off since the state had moved Josh to the Mansfield Correctional Institution. Maggie and the other women had moved to Mansfield to be near Josh. With Krystal's help, they'd rented a two-story apartment as close to the prison as they could get. Mansfield housed all the Death Row prisoners while they awaited execution.

But now the wait was over. Josh

had been transferred to the Southern Ohio Correctional Facility in Lucasville, commonly known as the Death House.

Maggie had never believed she could grow so close to a group of women. They'd worked together to try to get a stay of execution, to force an appeal, to do anything they could for Josh. Krystal had met with the governor's wife, a woman who believed in Josh. But the governor still refused to talk to them.

Nothing had worked. So here they were on the day of Joshua Davidson's execution.

Maggie stood in front of the mirror and stared at herself. She'd put on the navy dress Krystal had given her. Now she realized she'd buttoned it wrong. Her fingers shook as she tried to redo it.

"Let me help." Jessica redid the buttons and tucked Maggie's hair behind her ears. "Tell Josh that we love him more than life itself."

Maggie nodded. "Are you sure I'm the right one to go?"

Joe Meredith, the policeman who had come to the bar with Representative Nicholson and driven Maggie to Columbus, had arranged for Josh to receive one visit before his execution. Jessica and the others had decided Maggie should go.

"It would be too hard on Josh's mother to see him in prison," Jessica replied. "And the men are out. I'm sure Jude would love to go and get fresh material for that book of his. Did you hear that he got half a million dollars for that ridiculous article he wrote? Don't get me started! Anyway, we can't send Pete or Andy or any of the other guys—especially since we don't know where they are—now can we?"

Maggie had a pretty good idea where the men were hiding. Matt had called her a couple of times from a motel west of Columbus. She missed him. She missed all of them.

"You need to go now, Maggie." Jessica took Maggie's arm and led her downstairs.

Krystal was talking with Joe, who looked more nervous, more scared, than he had that day in the bar in Slayton. At the bottom of the stairs, Krystal caught Maggie in a giant hug. "Give Josh our love. Tell him . . . I don't know what to tell him." When she broke down sobbing, Jessica put her arms around Krystal.

Maggie followed Joe to his police car and got in. Joe had to tell her to fasten her seat belt. She couldn't think straight. Nothing seemed real.

"I have to pull myself together," she muttered.

The last thing she wanted was to make things worse for Josh. She needed to be strong, to carry all of the messages of love with her and give them to Josh.

"You can do this, Maggie," Joe said. His eyes were bloodshot, and Maggie thought he looked twenty pounds thinner than when she'd seen him last. He was probably putting himself in danger, just driving her to see Josh.

"Joe, we can't thank you enough for arranging this."

He checked the rearview mirror longer than he would have needed to if all he was worried about was another car. "Thank Representative Nicholson. He pulled every string and called in every favor and then some to get you this visit."

"Good for him." Maggie was grateful, and she was glad for Nicholson, too. It meant that he was still standing strong for Josh. She wanted to remember to tell Josh.

Joe slowed to let another police car pass him. Then he took a sharp left onto the highway that led to Lucasville. "Maggie, I need to tell you something. You have to be prepared for what you're going to see down there."

Maggie's stomach twisted, and for a minute she was afraid she was going to be sick. "Tell me, Joe."

"He's in real bad shape, Maggie. Real bad. It's not just the inmates. It's the guards. They beat him. They've been taking him out of his cellblock and having their own kind of sick fun with him. I know a guard, a corridor officer in J-block down in Lucasville. He said that last night, when they moved Josh to the waiting cell, the other guards blindfolded him and took turns hitting him. Then they'd laugh and ask him to tell the past—who'd hit him. And then the future—who was going to hit him next."

Tears burned in Maggie's eyes. How could they do that? How could they do that to Josh, of all people?

Joe and Maggie didn't talk much for the rest of the trip. Maggie watched the land grow more hilly as they drove south. Lucasville was situated near the Ohio River, at the northwest edge of Appalachia. Maggie had always wanted to explore southern Ohio . . . but not like this.

When they reached the prison, Joe did everything he could to shield Maggie from the mob scene outside. But the crowd was out of control. They waved placards demanding *Death to the Terrorist!*, *Where's Your Power Now?!* and *Save Yourself!* Men, women, and children spat at the car as Joe drove through the prison gates.

Maggie stayed as close to Joe as she could. As they ran in from the parking lot, flashes went off, and reporters shouted questions at them. They had to pass through a gauntlet of debris thrown from all sides. National guard and highway patrol officers had been called in to help manage the crowd gathered outside the prison. Maggie kept her head down and stayed as close to Joe as possible, darting into the building just as someone threw a beer can at her. It struck the door behind her.

Inside the facility wasn't much better than outside. The guards on duty glared at them. Maggie didn't set off the detectors, but two guards approached her as if she had.

The taller guard had a pockmarked face and a beer belly. His brown shirt rippled around his belt, and Maggie could see that a button was missing. "We're going to need to conduct a full search." He eyed Maggie like the men in the bar used to.

"Is that really necessary?" Joe asked.

"We have our orders. Step aside." The pockmarked guard pointed to a curtained area a few feet away.

Maggie followed him, her heart pounding. She hated the looks he shot back at her. The guard opened the curtain to the search room, which looked like a large shower stall. A female guard was waiting in back of a white table, the only piece of furniture in the stall.

Maggie stepped inside, expecting the male guard to stay outside. Instead he stepped in with her and drew the curtain around them. The female guard outweighed Maggie by at least 50 pounds and looked like she could handle herself. She pulled on plastic gloves and glanced over at Maggie for the first time.

Behind her, Maggie heard the snap of plastic. She

swiveled and saw that the guard also was putting on gloves. She caught the look of surprise on the female guard's face and knew this was no ordinary search.

"Strip!" The pockmarked guard's lips curled as he said it. "Now!"

Maggie wanted to bolt, to run out of there as fast as she could. She thought of the men she'd known, the men who had used her. That life was over.

"You heard me!" he insisted. "I told you to strip. If you want to see that killer, you'll do what I tell you to do."

"No," Maggie said quietly.

She turned to the female guard. There was no sympathy there. But the woman obviously wasn't enjoying this game.

"Let me do my job," the woman said to her fellow guard.

"I have my orders!" he roared. He stormed over to Maggie and began searching her roughly. She felt his hands start at her feet. She winced as he squeezed her injured ankle. When his hands moved up under her dress, she shut her eyes.

Josh has forgiven me. Josh has cleansed me. I am clean.

No matter what this man did to her, she belonged to Josh now. And no one could make her feel dirty, ever again.

When it was over, the guard seemed disappointed. "Go on! Get out!" he shouted, shoving her out of the cubicle.

Joe ran to her and kept her from losing her balance and falling. "Maggie? Are you okay?"

She nodded. She *was* okay. In some way she didn't understand, Maggie hadn't been alone in there. Josh's spirit had been with her. "Take me to him, Joe."

She followed Joe to a back stairwell.

"There are two other prisoners waiting to be executed,"

Joe explained as they wound down a flight of cement steps. "They're in the cells next to Josh. They're dangerous, Maggie. Watch yourself. Don't get close to their cells."

Maggie shivered as they exited the stairwell and shuffled through a cold, damp passageway. Joe unlocked a set of bars, then hit a series of switches on a wall box to open the barred gate.

Water was dripping from somewhere, making a steady, irritating *plink, plink, plink*. Maggie heard the *scritch scratch* of mice. Or rats. There was a dank smell of rotting flesh and death. Bile rose in her throat.

Joe stopped and faced her. "I can only give you five minutes, Maggie." He nodded, then left, locking the barred gate behind him.

Maggie turned around, and there was Josh. He was in the center cell, lying on a narrow cot behind the iron bars. His eyes were closed. The sight of him calmed her. She remembered how peacefully he'd slept in the back of the pickup, while the rest of them had been crazy with fear over the tornado.

Josh got up and met her at the front of his cell. Through the bars, Maggie could see that he was bone thin. His face was swollen, his eyes slits in purple lumps of flesh. Dried blood caked his hair. The front of his prison suit was covered in blood.

Maggie's eyes blurred. Her legs felt weak.

"Maggie."

She heard him saying her name. Calling her. *Maggie.* His voice cut through to her soul, giving her strength.

One of the inmates, an obese man with a scar carved

into his cheek, whistled at her. Then he turned to Josh. "Hey, man! If you're God's Son, let's see some saving right now!" He let out a harsh, cold laugh, then convulsed in a coughing fit. When he could talk, he spit out the words: "Come on, *God*! Zap yourself out of here and take us with you!"

The wiry man in the other cell shouted over, "Stop it! Aren't you even afraid of God? You and I deserve everything we're getting. But this guy hasn't done anything wrong!" The man lowered his voice, and Maggie saw tears in his eyes. "Joshua, when you come into your kingdom, will you remember me?"

Josh smiled at the man. "I promise that you're going to be with me in heaven."

Maggie couldn't help grinning. Even here, even in his last minutes, Josh had been talking to this man about his Father.

She tried to remember everything she wanted to tell Josh, but her thoughts were jumbled. Chance kept coming to her mind. She and Josh had never talked directly about Chance. She wished they had. And now it was too late.

"You'll be fine, Maggie."

She stared at his battered, scarred face and struggled to hold in her emotions. "Josh, I'm so sorry."

It was the most unfair thing that had ever happened, to do this to Josh. And he was letting it happen. He hadn't fought during his trial, and he wasn't fighting now.

"You could still keep them from doing this to you!" Maggie cried, swiping at her tears.

Josh smiled at her. "Maggie, they're not taking my life.

Dandi Daley Mackall

I'm giving it . . . so that you'll have another chance. So that everyone will have another *chance*."

"A *chance*?" Maggie repeated.

He nodded, smiling, holding her in his gaze.

And she knew. *He* knew.

"Let it go, Maggie. Let him go."

Back up the passageway, the barred gate clanged open.

"No!" Maggie couldn't believe her time was up. "Josh! I can't leave! Not yet!"

Josh showed no trace of panic or worry. "I'll see you soon, Maggie. I'll see you in Columbus after I rise again. You have another chance."

Joe was by Maggie's side, saying something to her. But she couldn't hear him. She was crying too hard. His hand clasped her arm, tugging her away.

The bars closed behind them. Through the walls of the prison, the words echoed.

Another chance . . .

Chapter Thirty-one

For the next four hours, Maggie
spent every minute on the phone. She
refused to leave the Lucasville facility
before the hour of Josh's execution.
She called every government office
in the state, trying to get someone
to pay attention, to listen to her. She
hounded the secretaries of senators
and representatives, but nobody
would talk to her. The governor
wouldn't take her calls.

There would be no reprieve.

At 11:30 p.m. a buzzer sounded,
signaling that preparations for the

execution had begun. Alone, Maggie walked toward the viewing room. Joe was nowhere in sight. She didn't know if she could bear watching the execution alone, watching them kill Josh, but she couldn't leave him. In the hall the shift commander gave her a hard time. He called two corridor officers to search her for weapons. They made her go through the metal detectors twice. Finally they let her pass.

Police officers were stationed at the viewing-room doors. One of them stopped her. "Are you sure you want to stay? This isn't going to be pretty."

Part of her wanted to turn and run out of the prison as fast as she could and never look back. Maggie thought about that day in the Community Hall in Columbus when so many of Josh's followers had done just that. Turned and run away. Josh had looked to his friends then—to Maggie, Pete, Andy, and the others—and he'd asked them if they were going to leave too. Pete had answered for all of them: "Where else would we go?"

Now, standing outside the viewing room waiting for Josh's execution, Maggie asked herself the same question: Where else would she go? This was where she wanted to be, where she had to be.

"I'm going in," she said firmly.

She took her seat in the front row, facing a large pane of glass that separated the viewing room from the execution chamber. Heavy green curtains were drawn over the window, which stretched across most of the front wall. The viewing room was small, with white-brick walls and a cement floor. About a dozen seats were set up, all facing the curtain. Maggie was the only spectator, except for the last row, where reporters were already filtering in.

Maggie didn't think she'd ever felt so alone.

"Maggie?"

She turned to see Jessica and Samantha. Maggie was never more glad to see anybody. She ran and hugged them. Then Sally walked through the door. And on her arm was Mary, the mother of Josh. Maggie went to Mary and held her. She was so proud of them for coming, so glad that Josh would see for himself how much they loved him.

"Sit down!" a guard barked.

There was movement behind the curtain, the sound of scraping, of wheels rolling, a rattling. Someone laughed.

Maggie led her friends to the front row, and they took their seats. She looked back at the door, hoping to see Pete there, or Andy or Matt. Surely some of them would show up. How could they stay away? Even if it meant being arrested themselves.

"They're not coming," Jessica said, reading Maggie's mind.

The curtain opened. Maggie's heart raced. Her breath came in spurts as she studied the execution room through the glass. It could have been a dentist's crude office or a small surgical theater. Everything was white. There were no pictures on the walls, nothing on the floor.

On a gurney in the middle of the tiny room a body was strapped, arms straight out to the sides, forming a grotesque cross of flesh. Every inch of the body looked bruised and battered. Blood still stained Josh's face. Maggie tried to comfort the others. She should have warned them, especially Mary. Mary's frail body shook, but she didn't look away.

Three people in white hospital garb studied machines attached to Josh. At the four corners of the room, prison guards stood at attention.

The warden was standing beside the gurney, at Josh's head. He looked down at Josh. "Do you have any last words, Joshua Davidson?" he asked, his voice gruff.

Josh winced as he turned his head to face the viewing room. Maggie knew he could see them. She thought she couldn't stand it. She could sense the pain that was everywhere, in every movement of Josh's body.

She could tell when he saw his mother. Josh smiled at her. "Mother, he's your son now." Josh's eyes flicked toward the door behind Maggie, and she turned to look. There stood Brad in the shadow of the doorway. "Brad," Josh said, "she's your mother now."

Mary cried softly, covering her mouth with her hands.

Josh glanced up at the warden and slowly surveyed the guards one at a time. "Father, forgive them. They don't know what they're doing."

The warden jerked back as if he'd been hit. He stammered, then gave orders to the people standing around the gurney.

A man in a hospital jacket took a large hypodermic needle and stuck it into Josh's arm. Blood spurted out. The man gasped, took the needle out and stuck it in again. Again, blood sprayed, then dripped to the floor. Two other people in white jackets rushed over. They circled Josh, their backs to the viewing room. Maggie couldn't see around them. Something was wrong. The guards moved in closer.

Maggie was aware of the reporters sitting behind them, whispering among themselves. Somebody made a groan, something like, "Ehhhgg!" and then said, "It's not supposed to go like this. This is my fourth viewing. It never happens like this!" Several of the reporters left the room.

Josh's chest heaved violently.

"Something's wrong," muttered one of the guards in the viewing room.

"My God, my God!" Josh cried out. "Why have you left me?"

Maggie fought the urge to run, screaming, from the room. She remembered Josh's warnings.

How he told them that he would have to die.

That he would suffer for the sins of the world. For *their* sins, for *her* sins.

That the Father would have to look away.

It was happening. And the agony on Josh's face was too much for her to look at. Of all the pain, the torture, and the humiliation he'd endured, this—this separation from his Father—was the worst.

The viewing curtain closed. They were trying to hide the debacle. But the curtain wouldn't shut all the way. Maggie could see Josh's body twisting in agony. She heard the arguing of the warden and guards. It was out of control. Things had gone horribly, horribly wrong.

Josh was choking, gasping for air. It went on and on and on. "Father!" he called. "Into your hands I commit my spirit! It's over. It's finished."

Then there was a stillness. An absolute quiet.

Nobody moved.

Suddenly the room went dark. Somebody screamed. Thunder rumbled. Lightning cracked. The building shook. There was a giant crash of thunder. Then the curtain on the viewing window ripped and fell away.

The generator kicked on, and light flooded the execution chamber. There on the gurney, arms stretched out at his sides, was the lifeless body of Joshua Davidson.

The warden nodded to the doctor in attendance. The doctor checked the heart monitor. Then he slid on his stethoscope and pressed the end to Josh's chest. He listened, then took the stethoscope away. The doctor, sobbing like a child, nodded.

The warden turned toward them and made the pronouncement: "Joshua Davidson is dead."

Chapter Thirty-two

Josh was dead.

The warden called for a lockdown. Guards ran around the prison, securing the cells. Reporters raced out of the viewing room, cell phones to their ears, calling in their articles for the biggest story of the year. Josh Davidson was dead.

Maggie and the women stayed in the viewing room. The generator clicked off and on. The lights flickered, then remained on. Maggie tried not to look at the mangled body through the window. She heard the sobs of the women around her and the shouts of the guards in the hall.

A siren blared inside the prison, blasting so loud she thought her eardrums might burst. Then it stopped. Over the loudspeaker came the voice of the warden. "Prisoners, stay where you are! This is your warden speaking! There's been a small earthquake. Nothing to worry about. Everything's under control."

Outside the viewing room, footsteps pounded in the cement hall. Guards shouted orders.

The cacophony of sounds blended together as Maggie stared through the window. She couldn't stop looking at Josh's lifeless body. How could he be dead? A part of her had hoped—believed—that they wouldn't be able to kill him. That somehow it wouldn't work on Josh. He'd sit up smiling, that twinkle in place. He'd tell them a story.

Through the dangling, torn curtain, she watched as four guards unstrapped Josh's arms and legs from the gurney.

"Maggie?"

She turned to see Brad behind her. Maggie reached for his hand and squeezed it. He looked years older than the last time she'd seen him. His mother, Sally, ran to him and cried on his shoulder. "I'm going to take Mary where she'll be safe." He came around to Mary's seat and had to lift her out of it, before leading her from the room.

Maggie glanced back into the execution room, but the gurney was gone. The room was empty. She sprang to her feet. "Where are they taking him?" she demanded. "Where's he going to be buried?"

A guard strode up to her and stood so close she could smell garlic and tobacco on his breath. "That's not your problem."

"Tell us!" Maggie shouted. "Or it's going to be *your* problem!" She wanted that, at least—to be able to go to his grave.

"So you and your friends can steal the body and tell everybody the great Joshua rose from the dead?" The guard laughed. "We know all about it. And it's not going to happen. So you can just tell your terrorist friends to forget it."

"Come on, Maggie." Sam took her by the arm. "He's not going to tell us anything."

Maggie tried to find Joe before they left Lucasville, but she couldn't. She hoped they hadn't done anything to him. Finally she let Sally drive everybody back to Mansfield.

Once they got back to the apartment, nobody wanted to go to bed. They stayed up praying and talking and crying.

"I want to visit his grave," Samantha said. She, Jessica, and Maggie were huddled together on the floor of the upstairs bedroom.

Sally came in with a tray of hot tea. "Bob and Brad should make a marker for the grave. We can't be the only ones who will want to find Joshua's resting place."

"Flowers," Jessica added. "We need to take him flowers."

"We'll do all of it," Maggie promised, surprised that her voice sounded firm and confident. But she meant it. She would find out where they were burying Josh, and they would all be able to visit his grave.

Thirty-six hours later, Maggie finally reached Joe Meredith on the phone. "Joe! I've been trying to get ahold of you. Are you okay? What's happening? What did they do with Josh's body? We've been crazy with worry."

Joe whispered, and Maggie hoped she wasn't putting him in more danger. "Listen, Maggie. It took a miracle, but Representative Nicholson and I talked the warden into letting *us* bury Josh. I have a plot in Garden View Cemetery in Columbus. We would have called you, but we couldn't let anyone know. That was part of the deal. That, and the armed guards Senator Harold stationed around the grave."

Maggie tried to hide her disappointment that they couldn't have been there for the burial. She knew Joe had done everything he could. She waved to Jessica, who was on her own cell, trying to get through to the governor's wife. Jessica hung up and came to Maggie.

"Joe," Maggie said, "we want to see where he's buried. We need to go there."

Joe coughed, then whispered, "I'll take you."

❖

Joe drove Maggie and Jessica all the way from Mansfield to the cemetery in Columbus. When they'd been on the road awhile, he asked if they'd seen the morning's paper.

"We didn't even watch the news this morning," Jessica answered. "I don't think any of us wanted to hear how much safer the world is supposed to be now that Joshua Davidson isn't in it."

"Then you probably haven't heard." Joe checked his rearview.

"Heard what?" Maggie couldn't imagine being shocked by anything ever again. Not in a world that would kill Josh. Nothing would surprise her in a world like that.

Joe glanced at her, then back at the road. "Jude Smith was found dead early this morning."

"Jude?" Jessica asked, leaning up from the backseat. "How did it happen?"

"He committed suicide," Joe answered. "Hanged himself."

Nobody in the car said a word.

Maggie didn't know what to think or to feel. She understood the kind of desperation that led to suicide. She'd been there herself and wouldn't have wished it on anybody. But Jude had betrayed Josh. He'd betrayed them all. And he'd ended up rich and famous.

And dead.

Maybe she was wrong. Maybe the world *could* still surprise her.

"Why?" Jessica might have been talking to herself. "Why would Jude kill himself?"

Joe shook his head. "Well, it wasn't money troubles. That's for sure."

Maggie pictured Jude the way he had been that first day he'd walked into the bar in Slayton with his camera. She hadn't known what to make of him then, and she still didn't. But she could imagine. Nobody could spend that much time around Josh and not feel guilty for betraying him. That was another thing Maggie understood—guilt.

Maybe Jude couldn't forgive himself.

Joe used his police siren to get them as close as possible to the cemetery. Long before they reached the front gate, Maggie saw army trucks and tanks. Dozens of police cars lined the street.

About a quarter mile from the cemetery entrance, an officer waved for Joe to pull over. The police officer approached their car, with two armed national guardsmen behind him.

"What's the problem, Officer?" Joe asked.

"We're not letting anybody into the cemetery today," he answered. "They buried that terrorist here, Josh Davidson. We're keeping a close watch for any kind of retaliation." He pointed behind him, toward the cemetery entrance. "National guards are posted at the entrance, and we've got the army and marines guarding that terrorist's grave."

Joe thanked him and drove off. When he was out of their sight, he turned the car around and drove down a gravel road to a back entrance. A dozen soldiers were patrolling the area. Joe tried two other entrances, but it was no use.

He dropped Maggie and the others back at Krystal's house in West Columbus. They insisted he come in and have lunch with them. When lunch was over, Joe said he had to leave, and Maggie walked him to his car.

"Joe," Maggie said, when they reached the driver's door, "thank you for everything."

She hugged him, amazed how much she loved this man. Not like she'd loved Ben or Chance's father. But then she wasn't even sure that what she'd felt for them had been love. It certainly hadn't been like this. Sergeant Joe Meredith was like a brother to her.

"I'll be praying for you, Joe. We all will." She let him go. "You be careful."

❖

Maggie wasn't about to give up on finding Josh's grave. The next day, she, Krystal, and Jessica took a taxi to the cemetery. But again they were turned away, this time by the marines.

Maggie worked hard to keep up the spirits of the other women. She got them to go with her to buy flowers for Josh's grave. They worked on a sign to mark the place where Josh was buried. They talked for hours about what they should put on it.

❖

Three days after the execution, Sally drove Maggie, Jessica, and Krystal to the cemetery. They left early in the morning, while it was still dark, hoping to get there before the police and national guard doubled their guard. This time they brought their flowers, arranged in the best vases they could afford.

Sally turned her van up the cemetery lane. "I don't see any policemen, Maggie."

Maggie was thinking the same thing. Two tanks sat on either side of the lane, but there was no sign of life inside.

Half a dozen empty police cars were scattered around the entrance to the cemetery. They passed the deserted police cars. Only one car remained between them and the cemetery gate. Sally kept driving slowly, all the way up to the gate. Nobody stopped them. She parked and turned off the motor.

"This is pretty weird," Sally commented, gawking around at the deserted grounds.

"You don't think they went for coffee or something, do you?" Jessica asked.

Maggie didn't care. Weird or not, it looked like they were finally going to be able to visit Josh's grave. She wanted to decorate it. She wanted it to be the best in the cemetery . . . in all Columbus . . . in the whole world.

"What number is the plot?" Jessica asked, already gathering up vases.

Maggie took out the map Joe had given her and showed them exactly where Josh had been buried. "It won't be any trouble finding it," she explained. "The rows are numbered."

Krystal was still surveying the cemetery. "Let's just hope that wherever everybody is, they stay there and away from us."

The sun was coming up as they scooped up the flowers and walked through the cemetery gate. Early sunlight turned the pale sky a bright pink. Clouds swirled across the horizon. A cool breeze made Maggie tuck her sweater tighter around her. She inhaled the scent of the roses and sunflowers she was carrying. They made her think of Josh's words about how magnificently God clothed the wild-flowers. She didn't think she would ever worry about what she'd wear again.

They walked right into the first cemetery lot without anyone stopping them. Dew glistened on the stubble of grass, sparkling in the first light of morning. Maggie still couldn't believe this. There was nobody in sight. The cemetery was quiet, deserted except for the birds in the trees. She heard a mourning dove call out, then another one answer.

"Where *is* everybody?" Sally whispered the question, as if she were afraid to wake the dead.

Maggie shrugged.

Jessica kept counting off the numbers of the plots as they made their way through the cemetery. When they reached the back lots, where the grounds ended at the foot of a hill, Jessica stopped. "That's it." She pointed to a plot set off by itself, barely visible under the shadow of tall trees around it. "That's where they buried Joshua."

Maggie double-checked the map. Jessica was right. There was no doubt about it. In that spot, maybe fifty yards away, lay Joshua, six feet under the earth. Dead.

For a second, Maggie didn't know if she could go through with this. Hadn't it been hard enough to watch him die? Did they really need to stand by his grave? Did she need this reminder?

Maggie closed her eyes and asked the Father for the strength she'd need. "Come on then," she told the women. "Let's do it."

They walked across the wet grass. Maggie kept her eyes on the grave. At first she thought there were two plots, side by side. One looked flat. Beside it was what looked like a fresh mound of dirt. Then she realized what she was looking at. "No!" she cried, running to the grave. "They can't do that!"

Krystal was hanging back. "What? Can't do what?"

Maggie ran toward the hole, the empty space where Josh should have been. There was nothing but a black rectangle there, a gaping hole in the ground. The grave had been dug up.

Standing at the edge of the hole, Maggie peered in at the coffin. The lid had been pushed back. The coffin was empty.

And the body was gone.

Chapter Thirty-three

Maggie didn't know what to do. She had to find someone. Anyone.

Jessica and Krystal backed away from the empty grave. The vases of flowers had slipped from their hands. Petals and broken glass lay in the grass. Sally stood on the other side of the grave, staring down.

"You look surprised."

Maggie screamed and wheeled on the man who had spoken. He'd come out of nowhere. She'd never seen him before. He was wearing white and sitting on the ground beside the empty grave. She wanted to ask him about Josh's body, but she couldn't get the words out.

"You're looking for Joshua, the one they killed," the man in white said softly.

Maggie managed to nod.

"He's not here! He's been raised from the dead, just like he told you he would be! Don't you remember what he said?" The man in white pointed to the grave and to the coffin, wide-open and empty. "This is where they buried his body. But he's risen from the dead. Go tell Pete and the others. Josh will see you all in the city."

Jessica, Krystal, and Sally were crying and laughing at the same time.

Maggie led the way as they raced back to the car. Josh had risen from the dead! He'd told them he would. He'd told them over and over, but they hadn't understood. It was too wonderful!

He was alive! Alive!

Sally's hands were still shaking so Maggie drove the van to a motel west of the city, where she hoped they'd find the men. They'd stayed in the same motel whenever they'd passed through Columbus with Josh.

"Wait until Bob and Brad hear about this!" Sally exclaimed. "I know my boys have had a hard time since Josh was arrested. But now—to have Josh back? Risen from the dead!" She was talking so fast that Maggie had trouble understanding her.

"It's too good to be true!" Krystal exclaimed. "It's a miracle!"

Jessica still hadn't spoken. Maggie looked in the rearview to make sure Jessica was all right. She was staring out the window.

"Jessica," Maggie said, "you heard what that man, or angel, or whatever it was, said, didn't you? Josh is alive!"

Jessica turned slowly from the window to look at them. "He really did say that? I wasn't dreaming? Josh is alive? Oh, Maggie! He's alive!"

They all talked at once then. Maggie had trouble staying on the road. She couldn't stop laughing. She wanted to call Sam. Everything was going to be fine now. Better than fine. Better than anything she could have imagined.

When she got to the motel, she knew it was the right one. She drove onto the lawn. Krystal and Jessica jumped out before the van came to a stop. Maggie and Sally raced to catch up with them. They dashed to the motel and knocked on every door.

Nobody came. Nobody answered any of the doors.

Maggie started over. This time she banged with both fists, while Sally went to the office and made sure that at least some of the guys were still registered.

"Maggie!" Sally called, running back from the motel office. "This is the right motel. They used false names, but I can tell it's them. They're just not here right now. What should we do?"

They were looking to her for direction. All Maggie knew was that she had to find the men and tell them that Josh had risen from the dead. The angel had trusted her. He'd told *her* to go and tell Pete and the others. And that's what she was going to do.

The restaurant.

Maggie didn't know how she knew, but she did. "Come on! They'll be at Antonio's." She knew they'd be together at the restaurant where they'd had their last dinner with Josh.

They piled back into Sally's van and drove to the center of Columbus. When they arrived at the restaurant, the building was closed for repairs. Part of the roof had caved in. It was too dark to see inside.

"Maggie," Jessica murmured, "I don't think they're here, honey. Maybe we should—"

"They have to be here!" Maggie answered. She ran around to the back entrance.

"Maggie!" Sally pointed across the debris-strewn lot. "The truck!"

Maggie looked. There was the white pickup, parked under a tree on the far side of the building.

The four women ran inside the restaurant, laughing, panting, out of breath, bubbling over with joy. When they rounded the hall to the private dining room, it was pitch-dark. Maggie tried the light switch. It worked.

"Maggie?" Matt came out from behind the door. He sounded relieved. "We thought—what are you doing here?"

Maggie glanced around the table and saw Pete, Bob, and Brad. They were all there—all except Jude. She realized they'd been sitting in the dark. Hiding. She was struck with a force of love for them so strong that it surprised her. Reaching out, she hugged Matt, then ran to Pete and hugged him too. "He's alive!"

Jessica, Krystal, and Sally were by her side now, all talking at once.

"It's really true!" Sally cried.

"We saw it with our own—," Jessica began.

"And nobody was around. It was like the police were zapped up!" Krystal added.

Maggie chimed in too. "The coffin was lying there, open!" She knew they weren't making sense, but they were bursting with the news and couldn't hold it in another second.

"Stop!" Brad held up his hand like a crossing guard. "You're not making any sense."

"Are you high?" Matt whispered to Maggie.

The question hurt, and for a minute, Maggie couldn't answer him. Matt's concern was real, and he certainly had good reason to ask, to doubt her. Still . . .

She shook off the hurt. It didn't matter what they thought of her. What mattered was what Josh thought of her. Out of all the people who could have received the honor of carrying this message, it had been given to Maggie. "The grave is empty. Joshua has risen."

Someone sitting at the table laughed.

Pete's eyebrows raised. When he spoke, it was as if he were talking to a child. "Maggie, that's crazy."

"Maybe you had the wrong plot?" Tom suggested.

Maggie glanced around at them. "An angel told us that Josh had risen from the dead."

Jessica stepped up beside Maggie. "Stop looking at us like we're crazy!"

"*You're* the ones who are crazy!" Krystal snapped.

Sally stormed over to her sons. "You boys listen to me! We saw that empty grave and heard that angel!"

Bob put his arm around his mother. "Mother, Brad was there when they killed Josh. So were you. You saw what they did to him. Josh is dead."

Sally yanked herself away from her son. "It's no use, Maggie."

Maggie had already come to the same conclusion. The men weren't going to believe unless they could see for themselves. She glared up at Pete. "The grave has been dug up, Pete. The least you can do is come to the cemetery and see for yourself."

Maggie hadn't seen Pete since the night Josh had been arrested. She could tell that he hadn't been sleeping. His face was unshaven, with a scraggly beard sticking out from his chin. She studied him and wished she could read his mind.

"He's alive, Pete," she whispered.

Suddenly Pete bolted for the door. "Come on, Maggie!" he yelled back.

Maggie ran after him, hurrying to jump into the truck before it took off. "Garden View Cemetery," she said, fastening her seat belt.

Pete hung a sharp left. "How did you find out where they buried him?"

Maggie explained about Representative Nicholson and Joe's help. Pete didn't say anything after that. Maggie thought she knew what he was thinking, though. He'd denied knowing Josh, and then he'd hidden out with the others. Maggie knew what it felt like to let Josh down. It didn't take a genius to tell that Pete hadn't forgiven himself. Maggie knew all about that too.

Pete kept glancing in the rearview mirror. Maggie turned around to see why. Brad was following them on his motorcycle.

When they got to the cemetery, Maggie told Pete where to park, and Brad pulled up behind them. She walked between them, winding through the headstones, until they stood within sight of Josh's grave. "That's it." She pointed to it. "That's Josh's grave. Go see for yourselves."

Pete took off at a jog. Then Brad broke into an all-out run and made it to the grave first. Kneeling beside the grave, he peered down into the hole. But when Pete got there, he didn't stop. He jumped into the empty grave. Maggie watched as Pete touched the insides of the empty coffin. He looked up at her with tears streaming down his scruffy face.

Brad gazed up at the sky. "He said he'd come back! Don't you remember? He said he'd rise again!"

Pete climbed out, and the three of them stood above the open, empty grave, not speaking. Maggie's heart tried to leap to the clouds. She didn't know what to do next or where they should go. She tried to recall the angel's message.

"He'll meet us again," she told Brad and Pete. "In the city."

Pete nodded.

Maggie wished she knew what Pete was thinking. If he believed her or not. If he believed Josh or not.

"Okay," Pete finally said. "Okay." Then he hung his head and walked back to the truck.

Brad started to follow him, then glanced back at Maggie. "Maggie? Aren't you coming?"

Was she? Maggie glanced at the grave again. She couldn't leave. Not now. Not yet. She shook her head.

Brad bit his lip, then kept walking.

Maggie stood beside the grave and breathed in the freshness of lilacs and newly mown grass. Closing her eyes and sitting cross-legged beside the grave, she called up memories of Josh, from the first day she'd seen him carrying out garbage at Matt's party to the last time she'd seen him, broken and lifeless, on the prison gurney. As always, her thoughts turned to Chance, and she held on to the image of Josh speaking Chance's name, explaining that he was giving her another chance.

Maggie understood that Josh had risen from the dead and gone home to his Father. She should be happy for him, not sad for herself. But the tears started, and she couldn't stop them.

"Why are you crying?"

Startled, Maggie glanced over her shoulder to see a man looking down at her. She didn't recognize him and supposed he had to be the caretaker. There was nobody else around.

"He's gone," she whispered, looking away.

"Maggie."

Maggie's heart stilled. Nobody said her name like that. Nobody except . . .

But it couldn't be him. She turned slowly and looked up into those eyes, those endlessly loving eyes.

"Joshua!" Maggie jumped to her feet and threw herself into his arms. "It's really you!" What she felt was so strong, so fierce, she didn't have a name for it. It was as if love, joy, and peace had melted into one emotion and flowed into every corner of her being, every spot where the emptiness had been for so long.

He held her shoulders and gently pushed her back so he could look into her face. "I haven't gone to the Father yet, Maggie. Don't be afraid of anything. Tell the others I'll see them very soon."

❁

Maggie headed back to the restaurant on foot, but she could have sworn her feet never touched the ground. This time she'd make them believe. Josh had spoken to her. She'd seen him. He'd trusted her with his message, and she would not let him down.

Epilogue

Dear Chance,

I can't begin to describe what the past few weeks have been like. We never know when Josh is going to visit us. It's funny, though, because it feels as if he's always here, even when we can't see him. Tom has seen him now, too. He wasn't with us when Josh came to the restaurant the first time. For a whole week, I think Tom thought we were putting him on. Then Josh appeared to him, too. Tom doesn't doubt anymore!

We've seen Josh several times since then. Pete had a hard time dealing with the way he'd denied knowing Josh. A couple of weeks ago, Pete just took off and drove to Toledo to play for the Mud Hens again. I knew he'd never be able to go back to the way his life was before Josh. Pete didn't do too well pitching his first night out, I guess. Then he heard someone in the stands shout to him that his fingers were spread too far on the ball, or something like that. Anyway, Pete adjusted his grip, and he started striking out batters one after the other. I wasn't there, but Andy told me that after the fifth strikeout, Pete threw down the ball and climbed straight up into the stands. Josh was there waiting for him.

Pete's okay now. I think he's going to do great—not at baseball. He's got more important things to do.

At first, I thought that this was how it would always be. That Josh would keep showing up when we least expected him. I don't believe that anymore. I think he's almost ready to go back to his Father. More like, we're almost ready.

Chance, this is my last letter to you. I know that Josh has forgiven me, and it's time for me to forgive myself. I need to move on to whatever Josh has for me to do while I'm still here on earth.

The next time you and I talk, it will be face-to-face in heaven. Josh is coming to you now. I'll be there when it's time. Then we'll all be together forever.

Dandi Daley Mackall

Maggie placed her letter into her pack with all the other letters she'd written to Chance. Jessica came and sat next to her on the hillside overlooking Columbus, while they waited for Josh. He'd asked all of them to meet him here at dawn. Maggie gazed around at the others. Matt sat a few feet away, blowing the white fluff of dandelion seeds into the air. Brad and Pete were laughing together. Tom, Krystal, Sally, Andy, and the others were all there. All except Jude. Maggie loved every one of them.

Josh appeared, walking up the hill toward them. He was smiling, drawing in the sunlight and sending it out brighter and warmer. They met him at the top of the hill.

"Go all over the world," Josh said. "Tell everybody about me and about the Father's love. And don't forget that I'll be with you forever and ever."

Maggie breathed in Josh's spirit. She could sense his love, his power.

And then he was gone. Maggie knew he wouldn't be back this time, not in the same way. He'd gone to his Father.

She reached for her pack and opened it. Then, standing on the crest of the hill where she'd last seen Joshua Davidson, Maggie lifted the pack and shook it over the hillside, into the wind. The letters to Chance drifted out of her bag and flew toward the sky. They floated away and got lost in the clouds.

Maggie watched the letters soar toward heaven as she let Josh's words settle into her heart: *"I'll be with you forever and ever."*

Check It Out . . .

If you want to know more about the real Mary Magdalene's life and the actual events that inspired *Maggie's Story*, read:

Chapter 1
John 10:10
John 2:1-12

Chapter 2
Matthew 9:9

Chapter 3
Matthew 3:1-6
Mark 1:1-7
Luke 3:3-6
John 1:9-23
1 John 1:9

Chapter 4
Matthew 9:9-13

Chapter 5
John 4:1-42

Chapter 6
Luke 5:1-11

Chapter 7
Matthew 18:12-14
Luke 15:1-10
Matthew 6:1-4; 20-23
Luke 6:27-36
Matthew 5:2-12; 43-48
Luke 6:17-23
Matthew 4:18-22
Mark 1:16-20
Luke 5:1-11

About the Author

Dandi Daley Mackall has published about 400 books for children, teens, and adults, with sales of 3½ million in 22 countries. In addition to *Love Rules,* she's written *Sierra's Story* in the Degrees of Betrayal series for teens and *Kyra's Story* in the Gold Medallion nominee Degrees of Guilt series for teens (both Tyndale). Her young adult fiction best sellers include eight titles in the Winnie the Horse Gentler series (Tyndale), including *Wild Thing, Eager Star, Bold Beauty, Midnight Mystery, Unhappy Appy, Gift Horse, Friendly Foal,* and *Buckskin Bandit.*

She was creative director of the teen fiction series *TodaysGirls.com* (TommyNelson) and author of *Portrait of Lies* and *Please Reply!* in that series. Her young adult novel *Eva Underground* (Harcourt) releases in 2006. *Larger-than-Life Lara* (Dutton/Penguin-Putnam) comes out in 2006, and *The Heart of Mary Jane* (Dutton) in 2007. She's also written three nonfiction books for high school students on having success in the workplace: *Problem Solving, Teamwork,* and *Self-Development* (Ferguson).

Currently Dandi conducts writing assemblies and workshops across the U.S. She writes from rural Ohio, where she lives with her husband, Joe, and three children—Jen, Katy, and Dan—as well as two horses, a dog, a cat, and two newts. You can visit Dandi at dandibooks.com.

DaVinci
DIDN'T CONVINCE ME

COMPELLING FACTS	CONVINCING FICTION

The Da Vinci Code: Fact or Fiction?
Hank Hanegraaff & Paul Maier

Divine
Karen Kingsbury

Jesus, Lover of a Woman's Soul
Dr. Erwin & Rebecca Lutzer

Magdalene
Angela Hunt

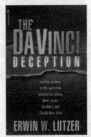

The Da Vinci Deception
Dr. Erwin Lutzer

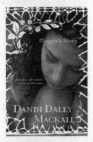

Maggie's Story
Dandi Daley Mackall

fiction.

thirsty

areUthirsty.com

degrees of betrayal

Sierra's Story 0-8423-8726-9
Ryun's Story 1-4143-0003-4
Kenzie's Story 1-4143-0002-6

degrees of Guilt

Kyra's Story 0-8423-8284-4
Miranda's Story 0-8423-8283-6
Tyrone's Story 0-8423-8285-2

THE LAMB AMONG THE STARS SERIES

The Shadow at Evening 1-4143-0067-0
The Power of the Night 1-4143-0068-9

other thirsty[?] fiction

Love Rules 0-8423-8727-7
Dear Baby Girl 1-4143-0093-X

areUthirsty.com

well . . . are you?